CW00541831

This book is a work of fiction. Names, characters, businesses,
organisations, places, events and incidents either are the product of the
author's imagination or are used fictitiously. Any resemblance to actual
persons, living or dead, events, or locales is entirely coincidental.

http://www.sofilaporte.com
sofi@sofilaporte.com

c/o Block Services
Stuttgarter Str. 106
70736 Fellbach, Germany

Editor: Julia Allen, Proofreader: Jessica Ryn
Cover Art: Blue Water Books

ISBN: 978-3-903489-02-8

The Vicomte's Masquerade

Georgians in Paris

Sofi Laporte

CHAPTER 1

alais, Late October 1774

C "Faith, 'twill not do at all. If we don't manage to find proper conveyance to Paris immediately, you'll miss your very own wedding, child!" Mrs Wilhelmina MacKay wrung her hands as she paced in front of a squalid harbour inn, the name *Le Cochon D'Or* fading in cracked red paint on a squeaking sign swinging over the entryway.

"But, Aunt Wilma, I *want* to miss my very own wedding!" Miss Melinda Finlay did not even bother to pretend to be the least bit perturbed by the dismal prospect of missing her own nuptials. Her lively dark eyes sparkled, and a tangle of unpowdered dark brown curls framed her face, on top of which sat a little rakish hat. Her oval face lit up with a gleeful grin. "In fact, I couldn't imagine anything more delightful."

With a groan, Aunt Wilma dropped onto the rickety wooden bench at the *auberge*'s entrance, causing it to wobble dangerously. The view from there offered a fabulous vista of the harbour and the sea, yet Aunt Wilma, preoccupied with worrisome things, could not appreciate it. "You've been harping on about this ever since we set forth from Scotland. May I remind you that you gave your explicit verbal and written consent to this marriage arrangement, and you promised your father to go through with this wedding. It's beyond my comprehension why you are so fickle now. Though I dare say it is entirely normal for a bride to be apprehensive and anxious on the eve of her nuptials." She patted Melinda's hands in a motherly fashion.

Could Aunt Wilma be right in that she was merely suffering from a case of the bridal nerves? For she'd like nothing more than to run all the way back to her home in Northern Scotland and crawl into her favourite hideout by Loch Eriboll. Since that was not feasible, she decided that any means of delaying the inevitable was good enough.

"Not that I blame you for feeling anxious. This voyage has been nothing but a series of disasters," Aunt Wilma continued. "First, we were delayed in Dover for over a week due to the inclement weather, then when we could finally continue the passage across the channel, both of us fell violently seasick. Then, lo and behold, we were told that the packet could not enter the harbour due to the low tide, and we were ordered to climb into tiny rowing boats from whence some watermen carried us ashore. The humiliation!" Aunt Wilma shuddered at the memory of being grabbed by a pair of rough seamen's hands, and without ceremony, carried ashore like a sack of turnips. "Then poor Betty slipped and fell in such an unlucky manner that she hit her head on a rock, rendering her senseless for an entire day. The girl will have to stay behind now, for we can't possibly wait for her to recover. How on earth are we to cope without our abigail?

"To add insult to injury, it turns out all our luggage has gone missing. Lost! Gone! Stolen! Causing a fiasco at the Custom House. And now we can't seem to obtain a private chaise to continue our trip. I really do not understand it, for John swore 'pon his soul that he'd hired one. That incompetent lackey is who knows where, looking for our lost luggage. Thank the heavens your *trousseau* was sent ahead well in advance and should have arrived by now. Your mother and your sister have fortunately already arrived in Paris. But both our servants are rendered useless to us. We *must* proceed without them. We must somehow hire a personal chaise, for nothing, I repeat, nothing will induce me to spend another night in this inn. It is an abomination. There are cockroaches, I say! Cockroaches!" Aunt Wilma pulled out a lace handkerchief from her pocket and dabbed her forehead with it.

"That's what I've been saying all along, Auntie dear. It's an ill-fated trip. Ill-omened, ill-starred, blighted, and doomed!" To underscore her point, Mellie stood up, lifted her hands to her mouth and shouted into the wind, "'Tis fate, heaven, and forces of nature that conspire to prevent this atrocious event, proclaiming, 'Melinda Finlay, thou shalt not marry the Vicomte Fouquet de Lacasse!"

Her words echoed over the sea, frightening a colony of seagulls and causing a gentleman walking along the pier to stop and give her a startled look.

Aunt Wilma flapped her handkerchief at Mellie. "Oh hush, child! Must you proclaim your sentiments to the world in such an uncouth manner? What shall people think? Everyone is looking at us. Promise me that you'll at least meet the man before you cause a scene at the wedding."

"If there ever is a wedding," Mellie muttered.

"What did you say, child? I vow my hearing is not as good as it used to be." Aunt Wilma rose and supported her lower back with her hand. "Ah, my back. Being jolted about in badly sprung chaises and lifted in and out of all sorts of vessels is taking its toll on my health. It is raining again. This weather is awfully dreich. Pestilential French weather! It's just like in Scotland. Let us have some tea in that dreadful tavern, if you can call that insipid brew that they serve here, tea. We shall have to ask that innkeeper again if he can arrange a chaise for us. What was his name again? Monsieur Grande? Minuscule?"

"Monsieur Petit," Mellie chimed in helpfully.

"Bah. Petit, Grande, it's all the same! The man will have to organise some transport for us. I'd be quite content with an oxcart or some other conveyance, as long as it has four wheels and moves towards Paris!"

Mellie followed her aunt into the inn's semi-dark tavern. It smelled of onions, smoke, and alcohol. Several rickety tables stood about haphazardly, occupied by weary travellers. Her aunt took the nearest one to the smoky fireplace. Above the mantelpiece hung a huge oil painting of an unruly sea with fishing boats bobbing on the waves like cork stoppers of a wine bottle. Merely looking at it made her feel seasick again.

"What now, Monsieur Petit? *Une chaise pour nous*?" her aunt boomed as soon as the innkeeper, a burly man with a moustache, stepped out from behind the bar.

"Impossible, madame." A string of fluent French followed, the gist of which was that it was out of the question. He swore on his soul that there wasn't a single chaise for hire in all of Calais. Not at the Cochon D'Or, not at the Hôtel Angleterre, and certainly not at Dessin's.

"*Ils ont tous disparu*," he said with a shrug. "All gone. Too many English tourists, too few chaises. *Que peut-on faire?*"

What can one do, indeed?

"But how can you give our chaise to someone else when we hired it well in advance?" Aunt Wilma complained, only to be met with another indifferent shrug.

"*Eh bien*, the chaise has been waiting for over a week. Madame has not been here, so I give it to someone else. Maybe in a day or two there will be some chaise available. You will have to wait."

"Waiting is what we absolutely cannot do." Aunt Wilma massaged her temples with a groan.

"We shall have to take the *coche*, then." Mellie dropped into a chair in front of the fire and stretched her clammy hands towards the heat. "How would that be for a bit of an adventure?"

"The *coche*! Certainly not." Aunt Wilma shuddered. "I have no taste for being jostled about in a wicker basket on wheels. Is there no faster means of transport?"

"But, Aunt, you just said you did not care for the conveyance as long as it had wheels," Mellie teased. "It might as well be the *coche*, which is no worse than an English stagecoach. Granted, it's rather slow and would take a week to get to Paris." She counted on her fingers. "As today is Tuesday, we will arrive in Paris on Tuesday next."

Her aunt sniffed. "Is there nothing faster than the bumbling stagecoach?"

"There's the *diligence*, which is considerably faster. But alas, Aunt, what are we to do? It left last night, and the next one leaves on Thursday. We could wait for it, of course, but then we'd arrive in Paris on Saturday noon, more likely the afternoon, for delays are likely. When is the wedding again?"

"Saturday morning," Aunt Wilma groaned.

"What a shame." Mellie took a sip from her tea with a satisfied smirk. "Missed the wedding by a hair's breadth. See, Aunt Wilma, regardless of what mode of transport we choose, it is simply not meant to be. As decreed by the heavenly hosts."

"Tosh, child, what nonsense you are spewing forth." Aunt Wilma poured herself from a teapot that Petit had brought in and took a sip, pulled a face, set the teacup down. "Petit! Fetch me a wee dollop of milk. *Un peu de lait?*"

"Bah. Here in France, one drinks *thé au citron ou rhum, pas avec du lait,*" Petit growled.

"The man is right. I changed my mind. Not milk. Bring some rum," Aunt Wilma ordered, which Petit was more inclined to follow. Back at the bar, he greeted a new guest who entered, bringing with him a gust of wind and rain. "*Une table, monsieur?*"

A gentleman in brown brushed off the raindrops off the sleeve of his coat as he looked around curiously. "*Oui.*" He stood indecisively in the taproom, casting a tentative glance in their direction.

"Why isn't your betrothed here to meet us?" Aunt Wilma demanded. "I vow I shall give that man a blistering dressing-down when he appears. It has been nothing but a disaster ever since we set our foot on this side of the Channel. How on earth will we ever get to Paris in time since there are no private chaises, and we can take neither *diligence* nor *carrosse*? So much could have been avoided if he'd sent us a chaise to pick us up."

Mellie studied her fingernails. "Why would he come here? Why should he care? I heard he is entirely indifferent to the welfare of others. As I said before, it's an ill-fated match."

Aunt Wilma huffed. "Poppycock. You know very well this was your father's dying wish, and he personally arranged the marriage before he passed on, God rest his soul."

Mellie set her mouth in a mulish line. "Papa was wrong."

"I do not understand why you are so resolute against your bridegroom. He is not only your father's friend, but a French vicomte. Rich, powerful." She ticked off each aspect on one of her long, wiry fingers, then paused with a wrinkled forehead as she searched for more adjectives. "What else? Did I already mention rich? They say he owns a château of considerable size. I forget the name. But they say the estate is massive. What more do you want?"

Behind her, someone cleared his throat. Probably Petit. Mellie ignored him and stared out of the window, where raindrops were tapping a rhythmic pattern against the glass. Dark clouds had gathered over the harbour, reflecting the mood that had settled over her. "There's plenty wrong with the vicomte. He is a terrible rake and a thoroughly wicked man."

"Fie, child! That's all hearsay."

"They say there is some truth in all rumours." Mellie shook her brown locks.

"Begging your pardon, madame..."

Aunt Wilma held up her hand. "Not now, Petit."

"I don't know what Papa was thinking."

Years ago, her father had arranged the matrimonial alliance between their two families. She had yet to meet her betrothed, for any formal presentation between them had been thwarted by the distance between them, in addition to a variety of other obstacles, not least of which included her own reluctance to meet him. Indeed, she'd actively avoided any encounters between them in the past. She was partly to blame for the awkward predicament she now faced as it became increasingly likely that she would meet her future husband for the first time at the altar.

Although she had initially agreed to the marriage, her consent had been given before she'd heard about the rumours. London's salons were abuzz with tales of the Vicomte Fouquet de Lacasse, depicting him as a person with a fearful temperament, entangled in all manner of political intrigues and scandals. He was a hard-hearted man with a voracious appetite for power and women—of all kinds. Then, there'd been that unsettling incident at the opera in London, which she'd rather not dwell upon. She'd almost come face-to-face with him there. Instead, she'd fled, convinced that she'd rather drown in the channel than marry him. To her dismay, that fate had not come to pass, though for a moment that possibility had seemed within her grasp when she'd thought she'd die of seasickness on the boat. But then, alas, she had a strong constitution and had recovered quickly.

"I hate him," Mellie said in a low voice that vibrated with passion.

"Who do you mean, dear? Your father or the vicomte?"

"Both. As for the vicomte, I'll marry anyone but him. I'll only do it over my dead body!"

"Oh dear. Begging your pardon—"

"What?" Both Mellie and Aunt Wilma snapped in unison.

The gentleman winced and took a step back. "I'm t-truly sorry."

"Who are you and what do you want?" Aunt Wilma barked. "And what are you sorry for, pray?"

"Ah. F-for interrupting." He blinked. "My name is—well, that is to say…" He swallowed.

"Well?" Aunt Wilma tapped an impatient finger on the table. "Speak."

The gentleman looked at her helplessly, then drew himself up resolutely. "If I may be forgiven for being so forward. Let me introduce myself. Brown is my name. Robert Brown at your service." He bowed so deeply that his wig almost flew off. He straightened it with one hand.

Aunt Wilma stared at him hard for one moment. Then her face broke into a smile. "A fellow Scot!"

He cleared his throat. "Well—"

"I can hear the accent. Scots are always welcome at our table, of course. Here, sit, sit, sit. Have you had tea yet, sir? No? Have some now. It is vile, and I daresay the coffee is better but only marginally. I recommend the tea, but only with a proper dose of rum."

Mr Brown pulled up a chair and sat down, casting a shy glance in Mellie's direction.

"This is my niece, Melinda Finlay. She's the apple of my eye. Yes, she is beautiful, but you needn't become moon-eyed over her, because she's as good as married."

"Aunt!"

"I would never—" he stammered, a blush creeping up his neck.

"Good. It is always better to say things clearly and without equivocation, to avoid any possible misunder-standings later." Aunt Wilma sniffed. "We can't have anyone falling in love with her, not so close to her wedding."

"Aunt!" Mellie clasped both her hands over her face, which had turned beet red.

"Here, have some rum." Aunt Wilma poured rum into

the teacup and pushed it towards him. "I daresay you look like you need it."

Mellie groaned. "I'm terribly sorry, sir. What must you think? Never mind my aunt. She is somewhat eccentric, but her bark is worse than her bite."

Mr Brown appeared to be rendered speechless. He dropped three lumps of sugar into his teacup and stirred somewhat absentmindedly.

Awkward silence fell over the table, except for the rhythmic tapping of Aunt Wilma's finger on the wooden tabletop. Mr Brown looked helplessly from Aunt Wilma to Mellie, and apparently having forgotten that he'd already done so, stirred two more lumps of sugar into his tea.

Mellie cleared her throat. Someone had to at least try to attempt to have a civilised conversation. "Mr Brown."

He sat up as if bitten by a beetle. "Yes. That's my name."

"So, you are a Scotsman, Mr Brown. Whereabouts exactly?" Mellie asked.

He thought for a moment. "Inverness."

"Inverness. Excellent. Are you on the Grand Tour, perhaps?"

He took a tentative sip from the cup, grimaced, and set it down with a sharp clink. "The Grand Tour?"

"Yes?" Mellie leaned forward in anticipation of his reply. A lock of hair fell across her face, which she brushed away.

He stared at her.

"Well?" Aunt Wilma's finger kept tapping.

"I beg your pardon." He bowed again. "I suppose I am, yes. On the Grand Tour, I mean."

Aunt Wilma rolled her eyes.

Mellie clasped her hands together in excitement. "Oh, I am jealous! I've always wanted to go on the Grand Tour, but my father said it wasn't for ladies. It's terribly unfair, don't you think, that only men get to have all the adventures? I would very much love to go on an adventure myself. It must be quite splendid. I've always wanted to travel and see not only France, but also Switzerland, Italy, and Austria. Austria is said to be particularly beautiful, and I've always wanted to see Vienna. Oh! And the Parthenon! And the North Pole, of course. Although one could argue that the climate there must be rather challenging, wouldn't you agree? Pray, what are your travel plans?"

He looked overwhelmed by her onslaught of sudden volubility and her sudden geographical leap from Greece to the North Pole. "My travel plans?"

"He does have a tendency to parrot one's words, doesn't he?" Aunt Wilma commented to no one in particular.

"I beg your pardon," he said with a bow in her direction.

"In addition to excessively apologising and bowing," Aunt Wilma added.

"Where will you go from here?" Mellie said. "Where are you travelling next?"

"To Paris, actually." He rubbed his hands on his thighs and took a deep breath. "If I may be so bold, I seem to have unintentionally overheard that you seem to have some difficulty travelling there?"

"Difficulty." Aunt Wilma snorted. "It's more of an impossibility. There isn't a single chaise to hire in this sorry town. Neither *coche*, *carrosse*, nor *diligence* will get us there in time, and we shall undoubtedly be stranded in this godforsaken place until doomsday, unless a miracle happens."

Mr Brown perked up. "Well, madame, let me be your miracle. May I offer you a ride in my chaise?"

Aunt Wilma beamed. "He seems to have some sense after all. You may indeed offer us a ride, Mr Brown."

"But we couldn't possibly, Aunt! It would be a great inconvenience to Mr Brown." Mellie looked alarmed.

"Not at all, madame, not at all. It would be my pleasure," said Mr Brown eagerly. "My chaise is well sprung, my horses are rested and swift, and I daresay we shall easily reach Paris by Thursday, if not sooner. It would be a more comfortable trip than in either the *carrosse* or the *diligence*."

A thundercloud settled over Mellie's brow. "But that won't do at all," she muttered.

Aunt Wilma stood up. "Perfect. Mr Brown, you have saved the day. I shall inform Betty and John immediately that they are to stay until Betty has recovered and John has found our luggage. Let us leave at once. I shall go ahead. Come, Mellie."

Mellie rose and made a move to follow her aunt. Then her steps faltered. She turned and sat down again.

There was nothing particularly striking about Mr Brown's appearance. He was a man of average height, with a brown wig and brown eyes. He had, Mellie thought, a pleasant enough face with an average-sized nose and an average-sized chin, neither particularly handsome nor ugly, but rather forgettable. His coat, waistcoat, and breeches were nothing out of the ordinary. His coat was wrinkled and brown. In fact, everything about Mr Brown was brown, Mellie concluded. She'd liked his somewhat shy, unassuming demeanour at first, but now she wasn't so sure.

She scowled at him. "And here I thought you were a perfectly pleasant person. You just ruined everything."

He gave her a startled look. "I'm terribly sorry." After a moment he added timidly, "though I am not at all sure what I am sorry for. What exactly have I just ruined?"

Mellie gave him a hard look. "I suppose your horses are awfully fast, sir?"

Mr Brown thought for one moment. "I suppose they are neither faster nor slower than other pairs of greys," he replied. "But we could certainly reach Paris swiftly and definitely before the *diligence* arrives."

"That won't do at all."

"It won't?"

"Most definitely not." Mellie crossed her arms. "Would it be terribly rude of me to refuse your generous offer? I really would prefer to take the stagecoach to Paris."

"But travelling in the *coche* is an unpleasant, excruciatingly slow experience."

"Precisely! It is slow. Very slow. I really do prefer slow, sir. You have no idea how much I would prefer it!"

He blinked. "May I ask why?"

Mellie thought. "So I can visit some places of interest? This is my first time in France, you know. The French landscape is supposed to be the most beautiful to behold! How would I be able to see anything worthwhile in a chaise that races past all this beauty? No. It must be appreciated slowly."

He scratched a spot behind his ear as if his wig was itching.

"Of course you wouldn't understand, being on the Grand Tour yourself," Mellie continued. "You can travel wherever you want and take as long as you need. But I—oh!" She placed her arm in a dramatic gesture against her forehead. "This is the only chance I will ever have to see something worthwhile. This is the closest I will ever come to having my own Grand—no, Petite Tour."

"Oh. I see."

"You do, don't you?" Mellie dropped her arm and beamed at him. "I knew you would."

He blinked and looked away.

"So, if you don't mind, sir, would you mind terribly if you left? Alone? Quickly? Now? Before my aunt returns. And take your blasted—that is, of course, your pretty—chaise and fast horses with you."

CHAPTER 2

He was, undoubtedly, a coward.

Philippe Alexandre, Vicomte Fouquet de Lacasse, had always considered himself to be pleasant and good-natured, and as a rule, endeavoured to be courteous and considerate to his fellow human beings, regardless of their status. He was usually mild-mannered and soft-spoken, never indulging in excessive emotion, never raising his voice in anger, and never being particularly demanding of his servants, whose lives in his service must be a daily challenge of toil and labour. He considered himself to be a humanitarian who was not mean-fisted when it came to philanthropy. To his surprise, he was considered quite a catch on the marriage mart— although he was rather shy—especially when it came to the fairer sex. Why the ladies still insisted on fluttering around him like butterflies was a mystery to him.

He fulfilled his role as a courtier with excellence only because he hid behind an elaborate mask of fashion and style and had a knack for acting. Versailles was but a massive, lavish stage, and he was one of the many actors on it. But apart from this eccentricity in his character, he'd had the impression that his fellow men found him tolerable and generally didn't hold him in excessive dislike.

There was nothing he could do about the reputation regarding his family name. Despite being only vicomtes, their family was one of the oldest in France. His father—and his grandfather before him—had ruled over the estate with an iron fist, and they were known to be feared well beyond their domain. Fouquet de Lacasse was a name that could make even the most hardened man knock his knees together in fear. For this reason, Philippe preferred to travel incognito.

He neither gambled nor drank, nor did he indulge in any other vice. He went to bed at a reasonable hour and got up when the sun rose. He enjoyed gardening and reading Homer's epics in Greek. He drank exactly one cup of coffee a day, with three lumps of sugar, and went to church on Sundays like any other good Christian.

Outside of his courtly disguise, he was, to put it bluntly, boring.

So it was with no small surprise that he'd heard his character being violently torn to shreds by a member of the fairer sex as soon as he'd set foot in that harbour inn.

He found it a novel and thoroughly humiliating experience.

His first impulse had been to flee.

Instead, he'd remained rooted to the spot, gazing with growing fascination at the dark-haired beauty who didn't mince her words in declaring he was the worst sort of cad to walk on the face of the earth, and that she'd rather die than marry him.

When his malfunctioning brain started working again, he realised she must be the same female who'd been screaming his name out there some time earlier. He'd been walking along the pier, watching the tide come in, wondering if he'd lost his senses and started hearing things.

It turned out he hadn't.

He'd gathered all his courage, followed her into the tavern, and approached the table she was sharing with a terrifying-looking woman with a narrow face, a pointed nose, and a hat that looked like a chimney stack perched on top of an iron-grey wig.

When both women snapped at him the moment he'd dared to open his mouth, he'd lost all courage.

For it turned out that this female was none other than his bride.

That made things somewhat awkward.

He simply could not bring himself to reveal himself as the man she so loathed.

So, in desperation, he'd given them the first name that came to his mind, which was that of his friend and mentor, a certain Mr Robert Brown, who'd been a professor of Natural Philosophy at the University of Edinburgh before he moved to France to become his personal tutor. Thanks to him, Philippe's English was excellent, and he could easily pass for a Scotsman, having picked up a bit of the Scottish brogue.

He really was a hopelessly cowardly dolt.

Philippe sighed.

"Well?" she asked, her hands on her hips.

Ciel, what was it he'd said now that had the girl glaring at him with narrow, hostile eyes?

He'd offered them a ride to Paris in his comfortable chaise. Was that such a crime? He thought it was the thing to do when one's bride arrived in one's homeland, to make sure that she was looked after and taken to her future home in safety and comfort. It was for this express purpose that he'd travelled to Calais himself, when he could have just sent a chaise. Should he not have done so?

She was beautiful all right, his bride. She wore a forest green riding habit of the kind that had become fashionable, not only for horseback riding but also for travelling, trimmed with mustard yellow velvet ribbon and lace that fell at the cuffs and at the neck. Her hair was unpowdered, and she wore a ridiculous little tricorn hat on her head.

His heart skipped a beat.

She wasn't beautiful, no. That was too common a word.

She was ethereal. One of those enchanting fairy creatures that belonged more to the flowers and forests, the kind one could never quite grasp.

But what he did grasp most clearly was that she certainly did not want to go with him in his chaise, because she did not want to marry him. Because she hated him. The vicomte, that is.

Mon dieu! What a fix.

It was too late to call it off.

The marriage settlement had been negotiated, the papers had been signed, the banns had been called, her *trousseau* had arrived. It would be a lavish wedding in the chapel at Versailles, followed by a banquet and a supper concert. The queen herself had announced her approval of the union, claiming she was delighted—no, she was enchanted and would be sending a wedding gift, and she expected his wife to be presented at court. A never-ending stream of invitations, balls, and suppers awaited them.

Given all this, their departure from Calais was imperative; if they did not leave immediately, they would miss the wedding.

When he'd offered her a ride to Paris, she refused, saying she wanted to see places of interest.

He saw through her ruse immediately.

He'd initially assumed that the delay in their trip had been due to inclement weather. Though this might have been partially accurate, he began to suspect that the chit might have done everything in her power to delay the trip. Missing the wedding seemed to be precisely what she wanted.

Since she had never expressed a desire to call off the wedding, this came as somewhat of a surprise. Was it possible she'd never intended to marry him to begin with? If so, why agree to the engagement, and why travel to France?

They'd already postponed the wedding once. She'd come down with the smallpox, they'd said. Then, her constitution had been too fragile and weak to travel. He'd been genuinely concerned about her health, for smallpox was a deadly disease that left many people disfigured. It would have been a justifiable cause for him to dissolve the engagement, on the argument that he could not bear to marry someone marred by illness. Yet, he chose not to. It was a matter of honour for him to remain true to his promise.

If she had ever been ill, she had recovered well, for the girl appeared healthier than a horse, and there wasn't a single blemish on her face to indicate that she had ever had smallpox.

Why had she lied?

A sick feeling assailed him as he realised that she might well be postponing the wedding for as long as she could, only to leave him stranded at the altar at the last moment. As the scales fell from his eyes, a surge of something shot through him, and he couldn't immediately decipher what it was, because he couldn't recall ever having felt that kind of emotion before.

He leaned back in his chair and drew his lips to a lopsided smile.

"Certainly, Miss Finlay. I shall be gone within the minute, taking my comfortable chaise and my trouble-somely swift horses with me. I wish you a safe trip. And ah, may it be arduous and slow, yes?"

"Famous." She nodded coolly and swept from the room.

No, it wasn't anger, he thought. That was too mild a word.

Rage, on the other hand, was too coarse, carrying an undertone of violence.

It was fury.

Pure, unadulterated fury.

Hitherto, he hadn't been too familiar with that kind of emotion.

But oh, how he welcomed it now.

CHAPTER 3

Heaven help them, this was the worst trip ever.

Mellie was squeezed between a sailor who reeked of alcohol and garlic, and a peasant woman who was sweating profusely. She held a basket of cabbages on her lap and would not stop talking. Every now and then, Mellie was jostled against one of them as the coach bumped along the road. Aunt Wilma sat across from her, groaning and asking every ten minutes when they would arrive. There were twelve passengers in the cabin, with several more sitting on top of the roof. The wicker baskets at the front and the back of the coach were overflowing with luggage, trunks, and boxes. Every now and then a trunk would fall out, which meant that the postillion, who rode on a pony beside the coach, would tell the coachman, who rode on one of the horses pulling the coach, to stop, dismount and fetch the errant piece of luggage that had fallen into the muddy ditch.

The whole journey was cumbersome and laboriously slow. Just as Mellie had hoped.

"Faith, I simply do not understand men," Aunt Wilma

groaned for the hundredth time. "Why would Mr Brown, who seemed a perfectly fine gentleman, offer us a lift and then, willy-nilly, disappear without a word? Did we offend him? Was he embarrassed by the poor state of his coach? Did he change his travel plans? I do not understand."

"He must have changed his mind and preferred a quiet journey to Paris, rather than having to converse with two chatty women the entire way." Mellie threw an apologetic glance at the woman as she bumped against her cabbage basket, nearly oversetting it.

"Humph. It is very ungentlemanly of him."

"Indeed. It is very unchivalrous and inconsiderate of him." A tiny twinge of guilt nagged at Mellie for discrediting poor Mr Brown's character. On the other hand, they would never meet again, so what was the harm?

"If we ever cross his path again, I shall give him a piece of my mind." Aunt Wilma gripped the leather strap of the window tightly as the coach drove through a rut in the road.

"That is unlikely. He's probably in Paris by now, with those fast horses of his." Mellie secretly thought it was a shame they wouldn't see each other again, because she'd rather liked him. He had seemed kind and somewhat shy, which she'd found endearing, and she would have liked to talk to him more about his Grand Tour. He hadn't tried to flirt with her, as men usually did, nor had he seemed vain and pompous, as so many male acquaintances had been. But why did he have to offer them a ride to Paris, instead of quietly going his own way?

Mellie sighed. Why could she not get him out of her mind? Why had there been that strange look in his eyes when she'd turned down his invitation to take his chaise to Paris?

And why did that still niggle at her?

"How much longer?" Aunt Wilma groaned.

"Five more days, Aunt."

They'd spent their first night in Boulogne in a shabby inn with unswept floors. Aunt Wilma had flatly refused to lie down on the rickety bed in the small room they'd been given, declaring that it was probably infested with vermin.

Mellie had not cared. She'd climbed into bed fully dressed, not bothering to remove her corset, bustle, petticoats, or shoes, and had fallen asleep as soon as her head hit the pillow. Aunt Wilma had settled into an armchair in the corner of the room, also fully dressed, and snored through the night, though she had declared the next morning that she hadn't slept a wink.

The inn in Montreuil the next day wasn't much better, only this time Aunt Wilma was so exhausted that she didn't mind sharing the narrow bed with the lumpy straw mattress with Mellie. Since they'd left their abigail behind, they helped each other in and out of their corsets.

At dawn the next day, they had a breakfast of weak coffee and bread. They'd hardly taken a sip when the postillion outside called for them to reboard the coach.

"Why this sudden rush when the coach is crawling slower than a snail to Paris?" grumbled Aunt Wilma. "We'd be faster walking."

Mellie was the first one to arrive at the *coche*, as Aunt Wilma had announced a sudden urge to visit the chamber pot. Rather than climb into the coach, where she'd be sitting all day anyway, she decided to wait outside and stretch her legs until the other passengers arrived.

Hearing a scuffle and a howl, she peeked around the corner of the house, where several boys were gathered, pressing against someone in their midst. One of them started kicking, and the others joined in until they were all delivering blows at a scrawny boy who was lying on the floor with his arms over his head.

Mellie thought quickly. She picked up a bucket of water by the wall and threw it over them.

"For shame!" she cried. "Three big boys against a wee one!"

The boys turned and stared at her like drowned rats. When she moved to pick up a broom to threaten them, they ran.

One little boy remained crouched on the ground. He looked up at her, eyes wide.

"Are you hurt?" Mellie asked the boy in French.

He shook his head.

"What cowards," she said in a scornful voice.

"They wanted to take *mon petit poussin*." He showed her a little baby chick he was holding in his hands.

"Oh, what a darling. You wanted to protect it, didn't you?"

The boy nodded. "I will raise it and never eat it," he told her. "So of course the others wanted it. Thank you for helping me, mademoiselle."

"It was nothing," Mellie began, then stopped as she heard a horn, hooves clattering, and a shrill howl of desperation that sounded like it was coming from her aunt. "Meelliiiie!"

She could have tried a little harder to catch it, of course. She picked up her skirts and started to run, and if she would have hurried just a little more, running a bit faster, surely the postillion would have called for the coachman to stop, and she could have climbed aboard.

She could have done that.

But she did not.

Her legs slowed until she came to a complete stop.

She stared after the *coche* as it rounded the corner and disappeared from sight. "Lawks. What now?"

While she generally had no objection to arriving in Paris later, she had not exactly planned to be stranded all alone at a seedy inn in France with neither money nor clothes.

The boy with the baby chick had followed her and stopped behind her, panting.

"Oh my, Mademoiselle, you have missed the *coche*! Because you helped me!" He stared at her with wide, frightened eyes. "What will you do now?"

"That's the question, indeed," Mellie muttered.

What on earth should she do?

Carriage after carriage pulled up. The ostlers ran to change horses, and there was a general bustle about the inn. No one noticed her standing there, looking somewhat forlorn.

She pulled on her lower lip thoughtfully.

She could catch a ride with the next *coche*. Except she had no money.

She could beg some private traveller to take her along.

Mellie shuddered. Her pride prevented her from doing so. Besides, could she really trust strangers? She was a woman, after all, alone and vulnerable. She was usually accompanied by a chaperone, her maid, or her aunt, and was not used to being alone on the streets. It was the first time she had ever been in such a situation, and in a foreign country, too.

It was her first adventure.

"The thing to do in a situation like this, I suppose," she thought out loud, "is to change my clothes." She looked at the boy expectantly. "Can you help me?"

"Anything, mademoiselle. For you, anything."

CHAPTER 4

Philippe's travelling coach was a Berline, a four-wheeled vehicle drawn by two horses. It was a plain brown chaise, without the family crest that adorned his other, more glamorous vehicles. He'd discovered early on that while travelling incognito might mean more discomfort on his travels since he wasn't treated according to his status, it also drew less attention to himself, which he preferred. He heartily disliked the fawning over his person merely because he had a title. And he dreaded the look of fear that crept into people's eyes whenever his name was mentioned. The rumours had always preceded him, all the way to the shores of England, it seemed.

Ah, what a legacy his father had left him! It wasn't the first time he'd wished his father and grandfather before him had been a little less domineering.

Philippe was enjoying wine and a plate of mutton and vegetables at an inn in Abbeville, when the *coche* from Calais pulled up outside. He'd arrived in Abbeville the day before, kicking his boots in the dust as he waited for the *coche.* He'd taken a walk around the town and, true to his role as a Scotsman on the Continental Tour, he'd bought a guidebook, read it cover to cover and dutifully visited the gothic church there. By the time the *coche* pulled up at the inn, he was thoroughly bored with waiting.

His plan had been to offer his bride and her aunt another ride to Paris, which he knew would now be more readily accepted, and they could still make it in time for the wedding. He thought of his beautiful bride, the mischievous sparkle in her dark eyes, and how his heart skipped a beat every time she looked at him.

She had professed to hate him, even though they'd never met.

She was quite prejudiced, his beautiful bride, wasn't she? Strong-willed, strong-spirited, stubborn, and spoiled.

His finger traced the rim of his wineglass. "I wonder if she needs to be taught a lesson?" he mused aloud. The idea amused him.

But after the *coche* pulled up at the inn, Mme MacKay descended from the vehicle without her niece. She looked round, saw him, and strode towards him. She told him in no uncertain terms that Miss Finlay had been left behind in Montreuil, and that everything was his fault.

"You should have given us a ride when you offered it," she said, smacking him in the side with an umbrella, "and not left when you did. All of this could have been avoided. Poor girl! What is she to do now, all alone?" She raised the umbrella again.

Philippe jumped aside to avoid a second blow. "But, madame!"

"Wheesht! Don't stand there, do something, you chucklehead!" she thundered.

He thought quickly. He would have to go back and find the girl. Mme MacKay could take his chaise and continue her way to Paris, and he would hire a horse and ride back. After he'd found the troublesome chit, he'd hire another vehicle.

Mme MacKay, visibly exhausted from whacking him with the umbrella, put up some resistance. "I'll wait here until you return with Melinda."

"It would be best, madame, if you did not. You could arrive in Paris by tomorrow and wait for us there in comfort, rather than spend a night at this inn. It is difficult to say how long it would take me to find her; though if the girl has any sense, she would be well on her way with the next *coche*."

"Sense! Bah. She certainly lacks that." Mme MacKay sniffed. "She is burdened with a more imminent problem. She has not a sou in her pocket, so she is stranded at the inn." Eventually she agreed to Philippe's plan and set off in his chaise to continue the journey, while he rode back to find his bride.

He stopped at every inn on the way and asked if there had been a lady in a green riding habit with brown curls. But the answer was always a resounding no.

Where could she be?

It was as if the earth had swallowed her up.

He arrived at the inn at Montreuil, but the landlord scratched his head and said he'd not seen Mademoiselle Finlay since the *coche* had left.

As he walked towards the stables, he wondered what he should do.

A little boy carrying a baby chick in his hands almost ran into him. His hands flew out and he steadied the boy.

"You didn't see an English lady in green, did you?"

Philippe asked the boy. "She missed the *coche* this morning."

"*Mais oui, monsieur,*" the boy replied eagerly. "I saw her. She is walking to Abbeville!"

"Walking! You mean, along the road?"

The boy shrugged. "Where else should she walk?"

Cursing, Philippe rode back along the road that he had just come, and as dusk fell, he began to worry. It was getting dark, and she had no money. Where would she spend the night? And what devil possessed her to set off alone instead of waiting at the inn? He broke into a sweat at the thought of all the dangers that could befall her. Beggars, vagrants, thieves, highwaymen... the list was too long to count.

He spurred his horse to gallop past a slow-moving farmer's cart loaded with barrels and crates. On the driver's seat, next to an elderly stooped man who held the reins, sat a youth eating an apple.

As his horse passed the cart, the youth threw the apple away, stuck two fingers in his mouth and gave a deafening whistle to attract his attention.

Philippe gave the lad a surprised look and slowed his horse.

"Hé, Monsieur Englishman. Looking for someone?" the boy asked in French. "You passed us at least twice on this road. You look lost."

He stared down into a pair of mischievous brown eyes.

"Or are you perhaps looking for me?"

Philippe opened his mouth to deny it, then he snapped it shut and nearly fell from his horse.

The boy turned to the old man, saying, "*Merci beaucoup* for the ride and the apple and the wonderful stories, Monsieur Barbet!"

The man took the pipe from his mouth and stopped the cart. "It was a pleasure, *mon fils*. It is rare to encounter a youth as courteous and charming as yourself. I would have liked to take you home to introduce you to my madame, for she would certainly have liked to keep you, as we have no children of our own to help on the farm."

The boy laughed, delighted. "I would have liked to continue my journey with you and meet your madame and learn more about the story of that terrible highwayman. But it seems my uncle has found me." The boy pointed at Philippe.

"Your uncle, eh?"

"Uncle?" Philippe said at the same time.

"My uncle. Since my parents are all dead, my uncle has raised me. You've been looking for me for a long time, haven't you?" The boy smirked. "I daresay he is very cross with me. Ah, he is a strict one! He wanted me to stay put in the schoolroom all day and study, but I could not resist, I had to venture out for an adventure. Do you think he will give me a beating?"

"You might deserve a little," Monsieur Barbet said. "For giving him a fright, for running off in search of an adventure as you did. But not too much, monsieur, for your nephew really is a most delightful fellow."

"No doubt he is," Philippe said weakly.

They said goodbye to Monsieur Barbet and watched as he drove his cart along the road until he disappeared.

Philippe looked at the boy. "Uncle?"

"I couldn't think of anything better to say. I suppose I could have said 'tutor', or just vaguely 'friend'. But I thought that there was a more interesting story behind 'uncle'."

The boy wore breeches that revealed a pair of long,

slender legs, and a threadbare coat that was too small. His hair was tied back and tucked under a cap, and he looked no more than fifteen.

Incredible, Philippe thought, what a difference clothes could make. Miss Melinda Finlay made a charming lad indeed. Her manner and entire being had transformed as well.

She snapped her fingers. "I have it! Instead of a nephew, I could be your page boy."

"I don't think so," Philippe replied. "As I am on the Tour, I would not be in the habit of taking along my page boy."

Miss Finlay thought for one moment. "Your valet, then."

"I already have one." He'd sent his valet ahead with Mme MacKay to Paris.

"Yes, of course you do. But only for now, for the duration of this journey. I think I would very much like to be your valet."

After Philippe had regained his voice, he said, "Give me your hand, and I'll help you up on the horse. We'll have to spend the night at the next inn, where I'll hire a chaise."

"I really wouldn't mind walking—" Miss Finlay began, but Philippe interrupted her.

"That is out of the question, mademoiselle."

"Yes, Uncle." She peeped up at him from under her lashes. "Also, my name is Max. Just so you know."

CHAPTER 5

Miss Melinda Finlay, now named Max, had had an entire room to herself at the inn. She dared not ask where Mr Brown had spent the night, for there were no other rooms available. Maybe he'd slept in the stables, or in an armchair in the taproom.

When she came downstairs, he was already there, rumpled and unshaven, pale with dark rings under his eyes. He'd discarded his wig, revealing cropped, rich brown hair sticking out in all directions, giving him a look that was oddly boyish and rakish at the same time. Mellie stifled an involuntary smile.

His eyes widened at the sight of her, then he passed a weary hand over his face. Now, in the light of day, he must have a better view of what she looked like than in the evening before. Mellie ran her hands self-consciously down the sides of her suit. Jerome had given her his brother's best Sunday clothes, consisting of a shirt, breeches that hugged her hips, waistcoat and coat, and a pair of buckled shoes. In return, she'd given him her own clothes to sell.

"These clothes are wonderfully expensive! With some luck, I should be able to get at least one louis d'or for them!" Jerome had said happily. "If not more!"

Now that she'd taken off the coat, she was aware of how tightly the clothes clung to her body. She'd left the corset on underneath, cut off her shift with a pair of scissors and tucked what was left into her breeches. Her hair was secured under a white wig. She did not know that she made a dapper boy, for she was tall, slim, and had good legs.

"Good morning, Uncle!" Mellie chirped cheerfully as she bounded into the room. "Did you sleep well? I am terribly hungry." Without waiting for an answer, she grabbed a roll from his plate, sat down, and munched on it.

"Ah, so I am the uncle again? The one who disciplines recalcitrant nephews? I thought you wanted to be my valet." He leaned back and regarded her with hooded eyes.

"I have come to the conclusion that since I spent the night in the room instead of you, it would be more logical for me to remain your nephew for the duration of our stay at this inn. Who has ever seen a servant stay in the room while his master sleeps in the stables? Is that where you slept, by the way? On a pile of hay?" She leaned forward, curiosity lighting up her face. "What was it like?"

"I didn't," Mr Brown replied with dignity. "I spent a rather uncomfortable night on that sofa over there." He pointed at a decrepit-looking sofa standing next to the fireplace. "After you have finished your breakfast, nephew," he emphasised, "we shall continue our journey in a hired chaise."

"There is no hurry," Mellie said, and reached for another piece of bread roll. She saw something flicker in his eyes before he turned to pour himself another cup of coffee.

She held the bread roll suspended in the air. "You are cross with me."

"Am I?"

"Correction. You are not cross with me. You are blisteringly furious." Her teeth worried her lower lip.

The tightening of his jaw told her that she was right.

"You are quite good at hiding your emotions, I find." She put down the roll. "You should come right out and tell me instead of being cold and quiet and polite. Don't mince your words. If you are angry with me, say so. Give me a good scolding. Shout at me. I have certainly deserved every ounce of your wrath, Uncle."

"Don't call me that." He looked as if she'd taken the wind out of his sails. "I'm not the type of man to rant and shout when I am angry."

"I thought not, but it would be better for you if you were. It is better for one's overall well-being to vent one's emotions than keeping them buckled up inside," she said sagely. "Whenever I am upset, I go to the loch near my home and shout out my fury and frustration. I know it is unladylike and shocking, but it helps. In general, I find it preferable for people to say what they feel rather than leaving the other party forevermore guessing." She picked up the bread roll again and buttered it. "I think I know what your problem is."

"You do?"

"Yes. You're nice." She broke off a piece of the roll, popped it into her mouth and chewed thoughtfully. "Possibly too nice." She finished the remaining roll in two bites.

A scoffing laugh escaped him. "In what way, pray, am I too nice?"

"The lame beggar boy outside the inn. I saw you slip

him a coin." She rested her elbows on the table, her chin in her hands.

He shrugged. "Anyone would do that."

Mellie shook her head. "No. Not anyone. Do you intend to eat that pastry?" She pointed to the millefeuille pastry he'd left untouched on his plate.

"You may have it."

Delighted, Mellie picked it up and munched on it. Then she went on, between bites. "Most people either ignore or bully the poor lad. And later, you were considerate of the innkeeper's wife, who is big with child, when you took the heavy bucket of water from her hands and carried it up the stairs yourself. I have never seen anyone do such a thing for the people who serve them. It is positively unheard of. And then you gave me the room, while you slept in the taproom. You also returned to find me after my aunt and I were rather rude to you. You didn't have to do this. You have no obligation to us whatsoever. You could have washed your hands of me, but you didn't. You've been a veritable knight in shining armour."

He cleared his throat, embarrassed. "Yes. Well. Seeing how distraught your aunt was, I couldn't help but step in and offer assistance."

She leapt from her chair and stood in front of him. "I owe you an apology, sir. I've inconvenienced you greatly, have I not, by embroiling you in my own troubles? I have taken advantage of your goodwill, disrupted your journey and exploited your generosity, and now you are delayed when you could be well on your own way." She gave a crooked bow. "I am truly sorry for the inconvenience I have caused, and you have every right to be cross with me."

"Oh, do stop bowing." Mr Brown glanced around the room.

"Didn't I do that nicely?" Mellie smirked. "I was imitating you. You like to apologise and bow too, in this manner."

Mr Brown looked flustered.

"It's very kind of you to go out of your way to find me and take me back to my aunt," Mellie continued. "Though I do not think it was at all necessary for you to ride all the way back here to find me. I managed very well on my own."

"So I see. That farmer very nearly kidnapped you and took you home as his own son. What would you have done then?"

"I would have liked that very much." Mellie smiled at him. "I find the French are all very friendly, don't you? I enjoy talking to them."

"Your French is excellent," Mr Brown remarked. "You could pass for a native yourself. I think you had that farmer quite fooled. He did not notice that you were no lad, nor that you were in fact a foreigner."

"I had a French governess who was very strict." Mellie wiped her fingers on a napkin and finished her coffee. "There. That was excellent."

"You have finished all the sweets, but left the savoury parts of the meal untouched," Mr Brown observed.

"Yes. I adore pastries, cakes, and sweetmeats of all kinds. But now I am finished. Let us go, Uncle. But there is no hurry, mind you. No hurry at all."

The chaise Mr Brown had hired was not nearly as well-sprung as his own, but it was certainly better than riding in a stagecoach or *diligence*.

Mellie chatted all the way about this and that, commenting on everything she saw on the road, pointing out the pastures and cornfields as they passed.

"Look! Isn't that village pretty? And oh, there are so

many beggars on the road. I counted at least ten of them when I rode in the cart with Monsieur Barbet. I felt terrible for them and wanted to give each one a sou, but I had nothing myself, except an apple that Monsieur Barbet gave me, and I could hardly give them a half-eaten apple. Have you seen the sights? Have you been to Abbeville? What do you want to see next?"

Mr Brown took out his guidebook and handed it to her wordlessly.

Mellie leafed through the book. "My word. So many interesting places! Shall we stop at Amiens and see the cathedral? And the gardens at Chantilly? Or even better, could we go to Rouen? The guidebook says the cathedral there is magnificent, and I would very much like to visit it."

"Rouen is not on our way, and we would have to make a detour to the south to get there. Your aunt will have reached Paris by now and is waiting for you most anxiously. Don't you think, given the situation, it would be best to get to Paris as soon as possible?"

Mellie shook her head. "I'm not at all convinced that this would be the best course of action."

"Not to mention the most important reason of all," he added.

Mellie looked up. "Which would be?"

"You are a single woman travelling without a companion. It would behove us to reach our destination as quickly as possible."

Mellie stared at him for a moment. "Oh. You mean my reputation." She pursed her lips thoughtfully. "But you see, that's why I'm a lad now. Your nephew. Although I think it would be more interesting if I were your valet."

He turned towards her. "That would hardly be fair to

my current valet, would it? If he were to lose his job so that I could hire you."

"You could have two valets. He could take care of your coats, and I could shave you."

An involuntary laugh escaped him. "We've already discussed this, and my answer remains the same."

"Why not?"

"Do you even know what valets do?"

"I suppose they are servants like any other," Mellie said.

"My valet looks after my clothes." He leaned forward. "He undresses me, bathes me, shaves me and helps me dress."

Mellie's mouth formed a round o.

"So you see, it is not at all appropriate for you to be my valet."

Mellie digested this. "You could dress yourself," she offered, "and I could help you shave. I would very much like to learn how to do it. I daresay I would be good at it. Better than your valet."

Mr Brown passed another hand over his face, and his shoulders shook with suppressed laughter. "Miss Finlay," he said after a while.

"Max."

"Max. I'm afraid you'll have to remain my nephew."

"That's a shame." She crossed her arms and sulked for a few minutes. Then her face brightened. "But, Uncle, if we can't go to Rouen, can we go to Rome instead, please?"

"You are a troublesome lad, Max. You are in need of some whipping."

"I ought to tremble in fear, but I am not in the least worried."

"And why is that?"

"I don't think you are the sort of person who would

whip anyone, not even a fly. You would open a window to let it out instead."

"How well you seem to have assessed my character these past few days, Max."

"Yes, I am an excellent judge of character." Suddenly, her eyes widened. "But pray, what day is today?"

"Friday."

Mellie sat up straight, as if stung by a wasp. "How can it be Friday already? How long will it take us to get to Paris?"

"At this rate, if we could increase our speed, you should be able to reunite with your aunt by evening, at the latest."

Mellie paled. "Oh no. This is absolutely terrible! Let's go to Rouen at once! I must see that cathedral."

Mr Brown hesitated for one moment before saying, "Would you mind telling me exactly why you are so reluctant to go to Paris?"

Mellie played with the tasselled cord that pulled down the chaise window blind. She debated with herself whether she could trust him. So far, he'd proved to be kind and reliable, even going out of his way to return and find her, when he had absolutely no obligation to do so. He was the quiet, reserved kind of man who preferred to listen rather than talk, and Mellie did not mind, as she could speak for both of them.

A strand of hair fell across his forehead, and his brown eyes studied her thoughtfully. They were kind eyes, Mellie thought. And they weren't just brown, but more the colour that whisky takes on when swirled it in a glass. Yes, she'd seen irritation in them, even anger, which was understandable. But an occasional suppressed twinkle also existed, as if he had a quiet sense of humour.

She liked him, she really did; and she decided on the spot that she would trust him.

"I suppose it would only be fair if I told you," she said slowly. "I have interrupted your travels, and you have gone out of your way to help me, earning only trouble for it. You see, I would very much like to arrive in Paris on Sunday. Or Monday. Or not at all. Perhaps we could just skip Paris altogether and I could accompany you to Rome and Greece?" She let go of the tasselled cord and the blind snapped up. "The truth is, I would very much like to miss my wedding."

Mr Brown looked straight at her. "Would you care to explain why the thought of marriage is so repugnant to you?"

She propped her arm on her crossed leg and leaned her chin on her hand. "I suppose it must sound odd."

"Odd's not the proper expression," Mr Brown muttered.

"The thing is, for some reason I cannot entirely comprehend, my father took it into his head to arrange this union. I was only a child, and he never asked me how I felt about it. He never told me so outright, but I suspect that this union is somehow intended to make amends for his fickle political loyalties in the past."

Her father had been a complicated man, full of contradictions. A Scottish laird who'd officially supported the English government to help him secure his land and fortune. In truth, he was a closet Catholic who'd harboured secret Jacobite sentiments. He was called a traitor by some and a hero by others. She'd worshipped him when she was a child, but that was before she understood his capriciousness, not only towards his country and his people, but also towards women. Mellie pushed the unpleasant memories away.

She twisted the cord of the blind around her index finger. "When I was younger, we had a good relationship, Papa and me. I used to think my thoughts and wishes mattered to him. I used to think that this childhood engagement was just a lark and that when it came down to it, he would not really go through with it. So, I consented. And suddenly, one day, he sprung it on me and told me the marriage was to proceed within a month. I hadn't even met the man I was to marry." Admittedly, she'd done her best to avoid meeting her betrothed when she'd had the chance. "And then, shortly before the marriage, Papa suddenly died." She dropped her head.

"I am truly sorry," Mr Brown said quietly.

Mellie blinked and shook her head as if to clear the memories. "After the funeral, I was informed that the marriage was to proceed as planned. It was my father's last wish. The settlement had already been negotiated and my trousseau dispatched. But then...I fell ill." She avoided his eyes. "The wedding had to be postponed. In fact, it's tomorrow." Her voice was tinged with resignation. "I am to wed an odious French vicomte. My father's reasoning was that marrying his daughter off to a Catholic French Jacobite would somehow atone for past events. It doesn't quite add up. But my father is no more. Therefore, sir, I must enquire: why should I go through with it?"

"Why should you, indeed?" he murmured.

"Perhaps that is not the right question to ask in this situation. The question to ask is, what can I do now?" She stared unseeingly out of the window. "I have decided that the only thing I can do now is to miss the wedding. Delay it as long as I can. Anyway, it wasn't my fault, the delay we had on this trip. We were held up by unforeseen circumstances. The forces of nature. That is all."

"I see."

She looked up sharply. His face was unreadable. "Do you? I'm not so certain. Most people reply along the lines of, 'But oh, it's your duty to marry him. Arranged marriages for economic reasons are what a lady of your status must expect. You must be an obedient daughter. This was your father's dying wish, so you must obey him.' Or: 'tis the fate of women to marry, and you must consider yourself lucky that you will marry one with a title. And oho! He is rich!' But you see," Mellie leaned forward and looked at him earnestly, "none of that matters to me. And though I do feel terribly guilty towards Papa, for indeed it was his last wish to see me married to his friend's son, I find that this sacrifice is too great for me. My father has lived his life. And this, this is my life, after all."

"If given the choice, may I ask what it is that you would have wanted instead for your life?"

A heavy weight settled on Mellie's chest. She smiled through a lace of tears. "Oh, I don't know. What choice do we women even have? Some freedom? Some adventure, perhaps? I have seen nothing of this world. I would have liked to travel around a bit, on my own, unfettered by rules, etiquette, and expectations. But this is an impossibility for women. So, I am rather enjoying that I can be a boy and taste some freedom through this ruse, if only for a wee while."

She rubbed her hand over her cheeks. Silly tears.

Mr Brown opened his mouth to reply, when suddenly the chaise gave a massive jolt. Mellie was flung across the interior and crashed into him, both heads smashing against each other with a painful crack. Then the chaise tilted sideways.

When she opened her eyes, she found herself lying on something pleasantly solid. It took her a few moments to realise what had happened.

She squirmed around, drawing a gasp from someone underneath her.

Blowing the hair from her eyes, she found herself sprawled smack across Mr Brown, both her hands on what she identified as his chest.

Three things flashed through her addled mind: One, that his chest was broad, muscular, and strong. Two, that she rather liked the way he smelled, for a whiff of citron and bergamot filled her nostrils. Three, that if she disregarded her throbbing head, this was rather...pleasant, given the situation.

Their eyes met. She was drowning in a sea of whisky brown.

"Are you hurt?" he asked.

When she realised that both his arms were wrapped about her protectively, a rush of heat went through her, and she struggled to get up, inadvertently smashing her elbow into his stomach.

He groaned.

"I beg your pardon," she gasped.

As she scrambled out of the coach, she banged her already aching head against the chaise ceiling.

"My poor head!" Mellie dropped to the side of the road, clutching her head, groaning.

Mr Brown crawled out after her and enquired once more whether she was hurt.

"Never fear, my head is stronger than marble," she informed him, rubbing her temple.

"So I noticed." Mr Brown rubbed his own head and proceeded to survey the calamity. "We have lost a wheel," he reported after consulting with the coachman. "The axle is broken, and one of the horses has injured its leg. The coachman will ride ahead to the next inn to get help, but in the meantime, we're stranded here."

Mellie looked about and found they were in the middle of the countryside, surrounded by fields, fields, and more fields.

"Congratulations, Miss Finlay, on the inevitable: now you will most certainly miss your wedding," Mr Brown informed her, cynicism lacing his voice.

CHAPTER 6

Mellie was in a splendid mood.

They walked side-by-side along a seemingly never-ending road. A cold wind blew, making her shiver in her thin coat, but thankfully it didn't rain. Ignoring the cold, Mellie whistled, skipped over puddles, and picked up sticks and stones along the way. Every now and then, she glanced at her companion and found him withdrawn and sullen.

Once or twice, she'd tried to make conversation. "The French countryside is pretty, don't you think?"

They'd seen some barren fields and were now approaching a forest.

He did not answer.

"Look! Isn't that cottage dainty?" She pointed to a farmer's cottage with stone walls and a thatched straw roof.

He'd not as much as glanced in the direction of her finger.

"Are you cross?"

He narrowed his eyes at her.

"Cross is an understatement," Mellie muttered to herself as she plucked a leaf from a bush. "He's piping furious." This Mr Brown was the kind of person who turned very quiet when angry. The thought made her uncomfortable; but, really, was it her fault if the chaise had lost a wheel?

"Look, Uncle."

He gave her a look that could have killed her. She threw up her hands in defence.

"Fine. Mr Brown, I understand you are angry at me for putting you in an uncomfortable situation, but be reasonable. Did I force you to come back for me when I missed the *coche*? I did not. You could have simply ignored my aunt and continued happily on your own way. Since you are not responsible for me, no one would have blamed you. Did I force you to hire a chaise with a weak structure that would break down in the middle of the road at the first small obstacle? I did not. Did I choose to walk that long, dirty road that you'd insisted on taking? I did not. I would've chosen the more pleasant path through the forest. It looks like we're lost. So let us agree that this is the work of fate, which is beyond both our hands. So, will you please, at least for the duration of this journey, put your anger aside and talk to me? Because I feel very uncomfortable talking to myself while you walk next to me in silence. It makes me feel like the worst person on earth. Do you need me to grovel at your feet as I beg your forgiveness?"

Mr Brown stopped and looked at her. "To be fair, that's not quite it," he began, then interrupted himself when a chaise rattled past them, forcing them to jump aside as the wheels sloshed through a puddle.

Mellie jumped up and down waving both hands, but the coachman paid no heed to her.

"Why do you think none of them are stopping? This is the seventh chaise to pass us," Mellie asked indignantly.

"Because we might be highway robbers." He slammed the hat he'd been waving back on his head.

"Humph. That doesn't make any sense. Do we look dangerous? Do we look like we carry weapons? Now I almost wish we did. I wonder what it's like to hold up a coach. It would serve them right." She thought for a moment. "Mr Brown! Maybe that's it! Maybe we should try holding up a coach—I suppose not." She broke off after seeing Mr Brown's long, speaking look.

Mellie looked down at her wrinkled, mud-splattered clothes. Mr Brown, too, looked similarly ragged.

"I suppose we don't inspire much trust, the way we look," she concluded. "But pray, why did we not stay with our chaise to wait for the coachman to return?"

"Because, according to my calculations, the next town should be within walking distance, and we'd be better off finding accommodation there than waiting by the road, especially as night will soon be falling. Ah. I think I know where we are. This looks familiar."

They reached a crossroads with a sign pointing to Amiens and another to Poulainville.

"Familiar? Why does it look familiar? I thought it was your first time in France."

Mr Brown took out the guidebook and showed it to her. "I meant, of course, from what I've seen and read in this guidebook. I've fairly memorised it. We must take the road to the right."

"No, we have to go straight ahead," Mellie argued.

"Believe me, it's the road to the right."

Mellie frowned. "I really don't know. It doesn't feel like

we should be taking that road. It looks narrow and untrustworthy. We should stay on the main road."

"The road to the right is smaller, true, but it leads to the next village. We should be there in five minutes at the most."

"I thought we were going to Amiens?"

He shook his head. "We won't make it that far. Better to stop at the next village and to find somewhere to stay."

"Very well, if you say so." Mellie walked on. "The most stubborn man I've ever had the misfortune to meet," she muttered under her breath. "More stubborn than a mule."

"I heard that, Max," Mr Brown retorted. "And you're the most hard-headed female I've ever had the misfortune to meet. I mean that quite literally." He rubbed his head.

Mellie grinned. "I suppose that's true."

An hour later, Mr Brown stopped. "It seems we're lost."

"I *told* you we should have taken the road straight ahead!" Mellie looked at him in wrath. "You have no sense of direction at all. Now what do we do? Do we go back?"

"I don't understand." He took off his hat and scratched his head. "We should have reached it long ago." He glanced at the low sun. "We don't have time to go back."

She picked up a stick and whipped it against the bushes beside the road.

He shook his head. "She really does act like a lad," he muttered to himself.

"I heard that," Mellie replied. Her stomach let out a loud growl. "I'm famished. I could eat an ox."

"We're in luck. There's a farmhouse." Mr Brown pointed to a small cottage in the distance. "Surely we can find shelter there."

"If you say so." Mellie watched him stride towards the

farmhouse. "If we do, it will probably be infested with vermin," she added pessimistically.

PHILIPPE'S CONCEPT of accommodation was a room with four walls, a fireplace, a bed, a pillow, and a blanket. Ideally, there would be a washstand with a pitcher of hot water, a chamber pot, and a table with a warm supper. Some roast beef would be good. Wine would be ideal. A good Bordeaux, for example.

What they ended up with was a barn with a haystack, a pile of woollen blankets, a plate of bread and a pitcher of goat milk.

He stared at the haystack, flummoxed. His companion had taken one look at it and burst out laughing.

"I don't see what's so funny," he said testily.

"It is simply when you think it can't get any worse, it inevitably does." She held her sides. "This is first-rate accommodation. And this supper!" She lifted the bread and sniffed at it. "It smells quite nice, actually. It's still warm." Without further ado, she bit into the loaf. "M-hm. It's good. Fresh from the oven." She took a long sip from the pitcher and wiped her mouth with the back of her hand and handed it to him. "Try it."

He took it cautiously, sniffed at it, and then decided to throw all caution to the wind. He was hungry and thirsty, and if goat milk and bread were all his stomach would get tonight, so be it.

She walked around the barn, chewing on a piece of bread, inspecting every nook and cranny. As she stooped to pick something up, he looked away hastily, realising he was studying her legs and shapely form more closely than might be considered appropriate.

He emitted a huff and suddenly found the air in the barn inexplicably stuffy and warm. He loosened his cravat.

His bride-to-be, Miss Finlay—no, his nephew, Max, or should he say valet? He no longer knew what to call her. This woman in boy's clothes who behaved more like a cheeky lad than a lady—he rather liked her.

She took off her coat.

"What are you doing?" he asked, alarmed.

"My coat is mud-splattered and moist." She arranged a pile of hay into a cushion and spread a blanket over it. She rolled herself into a woollen blanket, dropped onto the hay pile, and curled up. "At least the blankets are thick and warm. I'm tired. Blow out the candle, will you?"

He stood frozen for a moment. Then he blew out the candle in the lantern on the windowsill.

"Mr Brown?" Miss Finlay's voice sounded small.

"Yes?"

"It's awfully dark, isn't it?"

"It is." He'd lost all sense of direction in the darkness.

"Do you think you could light the candle again?" She hesitated before adding, "It's terrifyingly dark, and there are frightening shapes everywhere."

"I shall attempt to do so," he replied. He groped for the lantern, found it, and, after several attempts, lit it with the tinder box that lay on the windowsill.

"Thank you."

Taking a big breath, he took off his own jacket and threw it over the hay a good distance away from her. Then, with a sigh, he lay down.

"It's not as uncomfortable as I feared," she said, turning sideways to look at him.

He crossed his arms under his head and stared doggedly

at the ceiling, where the light cast interesting flickering shadows.

"Mr Brown?"

"Hmm?"

"Are you still very cross at me?"

Ciel, how could one remain cross when she asked like that? How could he explain to her that it was his pride that was smarting? And that he cared little for her whoop of delight when he'd declared, earlier in the day, that she was going to miss her wedding?

His wedding. Their wedding. Bah!

She'd been in a chipper mood the entire day because she did not have to marry him... yet. It grated on him, even though he'd begun to understand the rationale behind her behaviour after her lengthy exposition on her father, and how she'd been browbeaten into this marriage arrangement. At the same time, he felt irritable at her insistence that he was a 'horrid vicomte' whom she never even wanted to meet in the first place. Not to mention the fact that the longer he knew her, the more he wanted to go ahead with the wedding.

How could he let her know he was that detested bridegroom?

He would have to drop the charade and tell her at some point.

Sacrebleu!

What a confounding situation.

"Yes, I'm still cross," he replied.

She sighed.

"To be truthful, I am more bothered about your complete lack of concern about this situation."

"You mean, how I seem to have no qualms at all about dressing up as a lad, spending the whole day with a strange man, when I am to marry someone else, and here we are together. In a barn." She sighed. "It's quite shocking, isn't it? Don't think I'm not aware of it. Expect the vicomte to call you out as soon as we arrive in Paris." She chewed on her lower lip.

He turned to look at her. "Is that what you hope will happen? That he will call me out for a duel? What better reason to call off a wedding, for the bride has eloped with another? No, don't answer. I fear what you might say."

"Mr Brown?"

"Yes?"

"I'm not that devious."

He hadn't really believed she was. It was his turn to sigh. "No, I suppose you're not. I suppose it's the contrary, and you act entirely on impulse without thinking of the consequences. And you have a complete disregard for any kind of social rules and etiquette."

"To be honest, I'm surprised about myself as well. I suppose my shockingly inappropriate behaviour these days is simply because I am all too aware that my days of freedom are numbered."

"You talk as if getting married is equivalent to facing an execution squad."

"It does feel like it."

The realisation of just how deep her feelings were about marrying him crushed him. He shifted uncomfortably to bring more space between them.

"Mr Brown?"

"Hmm?"

It looked like she wouldn't say anything at all for a moment. Then, when he thought she had fallen asleep, she propped herself up on her elbow and regarded him thoughtfully. "Haven't you ever wanted something with all your heart and everyone said you couldn't have it? Not sweetmeats or other silly material things. I mean, a desire that comes from the soul."

He thought for a moment. He'd always been given everything he wanted, so to him, the question was moot. But a desire that grew from the soul...

"Something that I wanted but could never have," he mused. "I suppose we all have that."

A memory from the depths of his childhood emerged. "I used to want to go to the seaside at low tide to collect mussels and go *pêche à pied*—fish on foot. Or hand gathering."

He'd seen groups of boys wading barefoot out into the soft mud of the wide beach to collect clams and scallops with a bucket or a wire basket and a small knife and shovel to scrape the shells off the rocks. He, in his satin suit, waiting in his father's chaise, had watched them with envy, thinking that surely there could be nothing more delightful than to join them, while his father had a long, boring business to conduct in the nearby village. Then, on a whim, he'd taken off his shoes and stockings, rolled up his satin breeches to his thighs and waded out to the group of boys. He never got as far as hand gathering any mussels, however.

Miss Finlay smiled. "Collecting clams and seashells during low tide; yes, that can be very entertaining, indeed. My sister and I used to do that as well. But we liked it even more when our father took us fishing on the loch."

He gave her a quick look. "Your father took you fishing?"

"When I was younger, yes."

"Then you are to be envied."

"I suppose your father did not go fishing with you or did not allow you to go hand gathering by the seaside."

He crossed his arms under his head. "You are correct."

His father's outburst of rage that day had been terrible when he caught his son wading about barefoot with the other fisher boys. The whole village had witnessed him shouting that he should never fraternise with the scum of the earth. At home, he'd received a sound beating.

He must have decided then that he had to hide who he really was, for it was safer that way. His true self was not compatible with his heritage and title. It would only cause trouble if he revealed his true self, his true desires.

Was that his soul's wish, then? To have had a freer childhood? To have had a father who took him fishing?

"Mr Brown?"

"Hmm?"

"Have you ever been in love?"

For a moment, he was lost for words. "I—what?"

She heaved a sigh that seemed to come from the depths of her soul. "I haven't. I am not at all sure what that is, love. I've read about it in the novels. But it seems rather vague to me." She sighed again. "I just think it is a great shame that I must marry someone I do not love at all. And he doesn't love me either. So I will never know what love really is." Her voice was heavy with sadness.

He'd grown very quiet.

"Mr Brown? Are you still awake?"

"Yes."

"I suppose that's why I've been such a nuisance to Aunt Wilma and to you." She shifted and rested her head on her arm, yawning. "Poor Aunt Wilma. Poor Mama. Poor Violet. They really deserve to have a better niece and daughter and sister..."

There was silence. Then, after a while, "Mr Brown?"

"What now, imp?"

"I am very sorry you could never go hand gathering. If you want, we can go together one day. Just you and me."

"I would like that very much, indeed," he replied softly.

There was silence.

"Max?"

A gentle snore was his answer.

CHAPTER 7

" I really don't understand," Mellie argued, "why you're so determined on going *that* way," she pointed to the east, "when I am certain that we have to go *this* way." She pointed to the west.

It was a sunny but cold morning, and her stomach was full of goat's milk and bread, and she should be in a splendid mood, but Mellie had been feeling quarrelsome and peckish the entire morning.

She dared not look too deeply for the reason.

Perhaps it had something to do with covering up a feeling of acute embarrassment that had been plaguing her ever since she'd woken up at the crack of dawn and found herself draped all over Mr Brown. Her head was pillowed on his broad chest and his heart had been beating a comforting rhythmic tum-tum-tum against her ear. His arm had loosely cradled her waist. He'd been asleep.

At some point during the night, he must have spread his blanket and coat over her, because she felt warm and comfortable.

Too comfortable. Her first impulse had been to snuggle

even closer to this most agreeable source of heat until Mellie became aware of their situation. She'd held her breath and remained frozen for several minutes. Then she'd slowly begun to disentangle herself and to bring as much distance as possible between the sleeping man and herself. She'd crawled to the other end of the room and nearly lay on the hard wooden floor.

By Jove! Her heart was beating so loudly she was afraid it would wake him up.

She couldn't tear her eyes away from him as the early rays of the weak morning sun played across his relaxed, sleeping face. There were strands of hay in his hair; his lips were slightly parted, and he looked young and boyish. She had to stop herself from reaching out and tracing his full lower lip with her finger. It was very tempting.

Her breath had hitched.

Even now, just thinking about it made her entire body blush, so maybe it was better not to think about it. But what on earth was that warm, tingly feeling whenever she looked at him? It was as if her veins were filled with hot viscous honey.

But, oh! Was she out of her mind? How could she allow this to happen? If the vicomte were ever to find out...

She pushed the thought away immediately.

It hadn't helped that he, too, had been in a strange mood the entire morning. He'd been distracted and there was an odd softness in his eyes whenever their eyes met.

Just like now.

Her heart jumped and raced, and she looked away quickly.

Mellie desperately looked around for something to quarrel about. Except, she found, it was terribly difficult to quarrel with someone who was so...nice.

She cleared her throat. "I am certain we have to go that way, for as you showed yesterday, you have absolutely no sense of direction at all."

He pulled out the guidebook from his pocket. "You may be right. But I want to go this way. It is the road to Charbonneau, which should be no less than half an hour from here."

"What's in Charbonneau?"

"A pretty *château*." He flipped through the pages of his book. "'*Château Charbonneau is one of the biggest and most beautiful châteaux on the Somme, with one of the largest estates in all of France. Originally a mediaeval castle, it was rebuilt during the Renaissance and lovingly renovated in recent years. The château is now considered to be a jewel of architecture and houses some of the most famous works of art, including tapestries from the time of William the Conqueror.*' We couldn't possibly be in the area and not see this place. What do you think? Isn't this what you always wanted to do? Visit places of interest?"

Mellie took the guidebook from his hand and read the passage in question. "Oh, how I would love to see it," she said. "But Aunt Wilma?"

He shrugged. "She's well in Paris by now. We could send a letter when we reach Charbonneauville to let her know that you are well and that she need not worry."

Mellie chewed on her bottom lip as she thought. "Very well. Let's do that."

They walked for a while in silence, passing by a small village with a church. The church bell tolled the hour.

Mellie stopped. With her eyes closed and her hands clasped together in front of her as if in prayer, she counted each chime of the bell as it rang through the air. "Four... five..."

"What is it?" Mr Brown stopped and gave her a curious look.

She shook her head. "Seven…eight…"

"Are you feeling ill?"

"Nine…ten." She drew in a shuddering breath.

"Max? Miss Finlay?"

She opened her eyes and looked at him in sheer misery. "It's ten o'clock, Saturday. I've just missed my wedding, Mr Brown."

Then she burst into tears.

THE GIRL COLLAPSED at the side of the road, drew up her legs, hid her face in her arms and sobbed as if the world had ended.

Philippe watched her helplessly. He crouched down beside her, but she turned away. Her whole body was shaking.

There were times when all one needed was silence. This was one of them. In all likelihood, this wasn't just about the wedding. It was about lost dreams, lost opportunities, a lost childhood. The sudden death of her beloved father, who'd betrayed her. The fear of a threatening, uncertain future married to a stranger in a foreign country. Philippe knew only too well what it felt like to need silence. When one simply needed to mourn.

So he sat down beside her and put an arm around her shoulder.

She leaned her head against him and wept.

After a while, a very long while, when her weeping stopped and a single tremor shook her body at odd intervals, he pulled out a handkerchief and handed it to her without a word.

She took it, wiped her face, and blew noisily into the fabric.

"You know, all this time you've led me to believe that this was a cause for celebration, to have missed your wedding, and that there was nothing that could have made you happier." He took the crumpled wet ball of a handkerchief back when she handed it to him. "You had me fooled."

She wiped her nose with the back of her hand. He handed her the handkerchief again, but she waved it away. "I'm sure you've realised by now that I'm a despicable person, Mr Brown."

"Despicable?" He raised an eyebrow. "I'd say that's a trifle harsh. Somewhat spoiled, maybe. Overindulged, and a wee overbearing—"

"Overindulged? Overbearing? You mean, as in conceited?" He did not see the glint of ire flash up in her eyes.

He thought. "Well, aye. Somewhat. Which is only natural for a young lady whose every wish has been read off her eyes since she was young...ow!"

She pushed him so hard that he lost his balance and toppled backwards into the ditch. "You call me arrogant and conceited?"

"You misheard. You are an angel, of course, selfless and innocent..." He scrambled up and ran away, while she picked up a stick from the ground and chased after him.

"Stop! Stay here so I can thrash you with this stick..."

But Philippe was too fast for her, and after a while both stopped and laughed, holding their sides.

"Look," he said reverently, pointing into the distance. "Look at this. The *château*."

ENTERING FROM THE FAR SIDE, they were greeted by a sweeping view of a park with long allées and symmetrically trimmed boxed hedges and trees, and in its midst, a magnificent castle adorned with colonnades, turrets, and a marble round arch portal. Its intricately crafted façade reflected in the glassy green water of a lake that lay in front.

The sun glinted off the windows, bathing the entire building in gold. "Beautiful, isn't it?"

"It is spectacular," she gasped. "I've never seen anything like it."

"Let us go and visit it." He led the way, grinning, immensely pleased with her reaction.

As they walked down the main avenue leading to the *château*, Mellie's pace slowed.

She tugged at his sleeve. "Mr Brown?"

"Yes?"

"Are you certain we're allowed to be here?" She glanced around nervously. "I look shabby in this wrinkled suit, and I haven't been able to wash my face or comb my hair, and both of us probably smell of the stables. This place is so grand, they'll probably boot us out the moment they see us."

He stopped. "The guidebook says it's open to visitors. But to be on the safe side, let me go and ask." He handed her the guidebook. "Here, you can read this while you wait."

He strode off towards one of the outbuildings, while Mellie sat down under the shade of a huge oak and waited.

She felt tiredness creep into her body. Surely, it was because she'd cried so much earlier. And because, in general, her spirit still felt dampened.

She couldn't quite explain why she felt so depressed. Her feelings were in a tumult of anger, resentment, and deep sadness. There was also a longing that she couldn't quite explain. And, lately, a fluttering sensation that confused her, as if the blood in her veins was racing through her body faster every time she caught sight of Mr Brown. And when he looked at her in that gentle way, she simply forgot to breathe. Her breath hitched.

She shook her head as if to clear it all away. "Pull yourself together, Melinda Finlay. This is nonsense. All nonsense," she muttered.

What was taking him so long? A good half an hour must have passed.

Her stomach growled. She was growing hungry again, thirsty, and tired.

With a sigh, she opened the guidebook. She skimmed over the section she'd read earlier about the architecture of the place. Its history was also impressive. The *château* and its estate were in the possession of an immensely powerful French family...

All the blood drained from her face.

Mr Brown took at least another fifteen minutes to return. By then Mellie had worked herself up into such a state that she did not know whether the best thing to do was to run back all the way to Calais, or to throw herself into the lake in front of her and to die there and then.

"We're in luck!" Mr Brown called cheerfully with a wave of his arm. "Not only is the housekeeper willing to give us a tour of the place, but we can also have a bite to eat. I don't know about you, but I'm famished."

"Mr Brown!"

"Max?" He came to a stop. "Has something happened?"

"Mr Brown! It is a disaster!" She could barely get the

words out. She grabbed his arm and pulled him back. "We must run!" She tried to pull him along, but he resisted.

"Why? What is it? Have you seen a ghost? You've gone completely white."

"This place! We must leave at once."

"But why? It's beautiful, and I'd very much like to visit the *château*."

Mellie shook her head wildly. "Out of the question."

"Max." He crossed his arms. "Unless you tell me what devil is riding you all of a sudden, I'm not moving an inch from here."

"Mr Brown. You don't understand. This is the residence of the Vicomte Fouquet de Lacasse."

His face remained impassive. "And?"

"You know."

He raised an eyebrow.

"*Him*," she hissed.

"I have no idea who you might mean."

She took a big breath. "I was supposed to marry the man today. He's probably waiting at the altar as we speak." Furious and ready to kill her.

"Oh. Him!"

Mellie buried her face in her hands and groaned. "Of all the bad luck! Why do we have to be here?"

He studied her closely for a moment. "Hm. I admit that this is somewhat—awkward."

She dropped her hands and exhaled loudly. "Somewhat awkward? Truly? This is a disaster. A calamity! An adversity of tremendous proportions!"

"I fail to see what the problem is. The man is in Paris. You are here, in disguise, under a different name. No one will recognise you. You won't meet. In fact, it's impossible. Why not use the time to look around, to rest, to have some of the refreshments that the housekeeper has so generously offered us weary travellers? We might even be able to obtain a chaise here. Come to think of it, it's an excellent notion and the least your bridegroom can do for you, unknowingly, of course."

"Out of the question," Mellie began, but Mr Brown was already striding towards the *château*.

"Make haste, Max," he called over his shoulder, and seeing her loiter, waited until she caught up with him. Then he took her firmly by the hand.

"Why is he so enthusiastic about seeing the sights so suddenly? He resisted it emphatically when I first suggested it," Mellie muttered as she scrambled to keep up with him, clinging to his hand for security. "Oh, heaven help me! I really, *really* don't want to do this."

THE HOUSEKEEPER, Madame Motte, was a kindly woman with grey hair pulled tightly back in a bun. She wore a dark green velvet frock and a cap on her head, and a key chain hung from her waist. To Mellie's relief, she smiled at them and did not seem at all put off by their dusty appearance.

"Welcome to Château Charbonneau. I'm so pleased to be able to give you a tour." Her eyes crinkled in the corners as she smiled at Mellie.

Despite the tour offering her a first-hand glimpse into the splendidly opulent place that would have been her new home, Mellie did not enjoy it at all. She feared the vicomte might appear at any moment, striding down the corridor, jumping out at her from a dark corner, or climbing out of a wardrobe for the sole purpose of frightening her.

She had to admit, however, that the place was breathtaking. She had never seen anything like it before. The king himself couldn't live in more lavish surroundings. One room was more magnificent than the next, decorated with gilded marble and elaborate floral carvings, the walls covered with silk and damask, the furniture delicately crafted. Each room had its own colour and theme. There were tapestries and oil paintings everywhere, as well as massive, gilded mirrors that covered the walls from floor to ceiling. The only room she did not like was the Hunting Room, full of the heads of dead animals, stuffed and hanging from the walls and even the ceiling. Her favourite room was the Oriental Room, overflowing with exotic plants and Asian furniture.

The current vicomte's grandfather, it seemed, had travelled extensively in Asia and the Middle East, bringing back all sorts of interesting things. He even wrote a book about his travels, the housekeeper boasted.

That particular vicomte, Mellie decided, seemed to have been an interesting sort of man. As opposed to the father, who seemed to have been a tyrant.

"The grand gallery," Madame Motte explained as they walked up the massive marble staircase, "is part of the old part of the house and dates back all the way to the 14th century."

Mellie marvelled at the sheer number of portraits hanging on the walls of a room that was so large it could hold the king's entire army.

"We also have family portraits here." She pointed to a row of oval paintings that hung to the right. They hung in pairs, a man's portrait next to a woman's.

"I suppose these are the vicomtes and vicomtesses through the ages," Mellie guessed. "I suppose they were all forced into arranged marriages, which is why they all look so disgruntled. If you were to put a pitcher of milk in front of them, it would no doubt curdle in the presence of so much sourness."

Mr Brown choked back a laugh, which he turned into a discreet cough.

"Ah. Speaking of marriage, today is a most joyful day, for Monsieur le Vicomte is celebrating his wedding in Paris. We are very much looking forward to welcoming our new vicomtesse soon," Madame Motte said. "Ah, these will be wonderful times, with a young lady here again, and surely babies soon. It will be a joy to hear the laughter of children again within these walls. It has been so long."

Mellie burst into a fit of uncontrollable coughing.

Mr Brown patted her on the back. "Are you fine, Max?"

"Yes, thank you," she gasped. "I must have mis-swallowed."

There was a slightly sardonic look on Mr Brown's face as he watched her regain her composure.

Madame Motte walked to the end of the gallery and paused in front of a portrait. "Ah, here he is, our monsieur. Is he not handsome?"

"What do you think?" Mr Brown glanced sideways at Mellie. "Does he look familiar at all, Max?"

Madame Motte looked at her with interest. "Never tell me you are acquainted with our monsieur?"

Mellie tilted her head sideways as she studied the portrait of a man of indeterminate age, with a large white wig, in ostentatious state dress, a sash draped over it, several gold orders pinned to his chest. His face was painted with a thick layer of white *maquillage*, a red spot on each cheek, scarlet lips, and beauty patches on his cheek. His eyebrows were slashes of black charcoal on a high, white forehead. He looked effeminate and insurmountably haughty.

It took every inch in Mellie not to cringe with loathing.

She had, of course, seen a miniature portrait once, and her reaction then had been the same. To Madame Motte she said, "Er, yes, I may have seen him once at the opera in London. He looked exactly the same then." But she hadn't exactly spoken to him. She'd only seen him from a distance, from her box, talking to an acquaintance who had gestured to her, and the vicomte had turned and made a flamboyant bow in her direction. It was the encounter afterwards that she'd wished she could forget. She bit down hard on her lower lip as she remembered the incident.

"But how wonderful!" Madame Motte pulled her out of her memories. "You're right, our monsieur has spent some time in London. This is where he courted his bride."

"That never happened," Mellie muttered under her breath.

Mr Brown gestured at the portrait with one hand. "Interesting appearance. Is this the latest French fashion?"

"*Mais oui*, our monsieur is quite a man of fashion," Madame Motte boasted. "He is a jewel in the court and a favourite of the queen. That is why the wedding is taking place in Paris, and not here in our beautiful chapel. The queen said she wanted to attend in person."

Did she? That was news indeed. Was Marie Antoinette pacing the church with her hapless bridegroom, cursing her for not putting in an appearance? Had she caused a diplomatic scandal? Were all English and Scots now disgraced because of her? What would happen to Aunt Wilma, and her sister and her mother? Would they all be driven out of the country, or worse, thrown into the Bastille?

Mellie broke out into a sweat. Heaven help her. What a

fix! She'd been so focused on escaping her wedding that she hadn't given a single thought to the consequences her family might face. Scandal and disgrace would hail down upon them. They would all become social outcasts.

For the first time, Mellie began to feel truly ill.

"Are you fine?" Mr Brown murmured into her ear.

I am about to be sick on the expensive Aubusson carpets, Mellie was tempted to reply.

"Yes," she said instead, through clenched teeth.

What was done was done. She had made her decision, and now she had to live with the aftermath. It was tempting to flee, but for the sake of Aunt Wilma, her mother, and her sister Violet, she would not, could not, be such a coward.

She drew in a shuddering breath and straightened her shoulders.

Madame Motte did not notice and chatted on. "I hear our new vicomtesse is equally beautiful. I am certain the children resulting from this union will—"

"Pray, let us move on," Mellie interrupted hastily. "There must be so much more to see!" She tugged on Mr Brown's coat and dragged him back through the gallery.

Madame Motte followed. "Indeed, there is so much more! Where to next? The orangerie. Now, the orangerie has a particularly interesting history—"

"You seem to think this entire situation is overly amusing," Mellie hissed at Mr Brown on the way down. "Don't think I haven't noticed you laughing and smirking behind my back. I am glad that at least one of us is having a good time, even if it is at my expense."

"Me? I wouldn't dream of amusing myself at your expense, and I certainly don't smirk," Mr Brown said, his lips twitching.

"Liar."

"Although I am beginning to understand why you are so determined to flee the altar. The man looks like a veritable dolt. Don't let Madame Motte hear I just said that lest she throws us out before she serves us tea. By Jove, I could do with a proper English tea tray. I'm rather famished." He put a hand to his stomach.

Madame Motte had gone ahead and told them about the history of the garden, the labyrinth, and the Greek ruins in the park.

An hour later, just as they reached the greenhouse, the weather suddenly changed. A strong wind came up, and it began to rain. "We must hurry back to the house," the housekeeper proclaimed. As she spoke, a downpour began as they hurried back.

"What weather! There, this is the end of our tour. I shall be happy to serve you some coffee. But, monsieur, I am rather concerned about your continuing trip. You said you wanted to travel to Paris? In this weather?" Madame Motte pursed her lips and shook her head. "I don't approve."

"Indeed, what a fix," Mr Brown replied. "What can we do?"

"I am happy to prepare you a room here for the night," the housekeeper offered. "Hopefully by tomorrow the storm will have calmed."

"Sleep here?" Mellie's voice was laced with horror. "Certainly not."

"Certainly yes. What a wonderful suggestion, Madame Motte. How very generous of you." Did Mellie imagine it, or did Mr Brown just wink at the woman? And did Madame Motte *simper* back at him? If Mellie hadn't been certain that the weather had caused this horrible predicament of having to spend a night at this place, she would have believed the two were colluding together to make it happen.

"Yes, well, since Monsieur le Vicomte and his bride won't be returning until at least a fortnight, it won't matter much. I am happy to offer you and your charming, err, nephew a room." Madame Motte jingled her keys, looking for the right one.

Mellie shook her head. "But—"

"Look at the weather, Max. Be sensible." Mr Brown pointed outside of the window, where the wind and the rain were beating against the glass. "It's a storm."

"It will have passed by tomorrow. Until then, get a good rest, and a warm supper, and I shall have your clothes washed and pressed, yes?" For Madame Motte, the matter was settled.

Mellie looked at her doubtfully. There was nothing she wanted more than to escape from this place. Having to spend a night in the walls of the home of her jilted bride-groom was the epitome of embarrassment. But what else could they do? Continuing their journey in such weather was folly.

"Very well," she said resignedly.

CHAPTER 8

Philippe had ordered a simple supper to be served in the small dining room situated on the lower floor. The table was exquisitely laid with a damask tablecloth, sterling silverware, and crystal goblets. They were served a hearty soup, roasted meats with a selection of vegetables, followed by an array of cheeses, grapes, figs, and other fruit, and pastries. The meal was somewhat simpler than his usual fare, but judging from Miss Finlay's wide-eyed astonishment, it was opulent enough to be impressive.

Madame Motte had executed her role well. He'd instructed his housekeeper earlier, of course, regarding their unique situation, requesting her to keep his anonymity and to play along. Miss Finlay had clearly appeared both intimidated and overwhelmed at touring her future home. He was glad to see that she appreciated its beauty, while simultaneously appearing to be somewhat awe-inspired. He was pleased to learn her favourite room was the Oriental Room, which was also his favourite.

Tonight, Miss Finlay would be accommodated in one of the smaller, but equally charming guest rooms.

He wondered whether she would like her own apartments, which he had taken great pains to furnish and decorate. Those rooms they had not visited, for they would be available to her only upon marriage.

Philippe sighed. Would that day ever come? He'd dispatched numerous letters to Paris from Abbeville regarding the subsequent procedure regarding their wedding. For the moment, the situation should be under control.

While they were being served, Miss Finlay's curiosity regarding the household staff became evident, and she asked the maid who served them all sorts of questions regarding her workload, salary and whether she was well fed and happy here. The girl answered all her questions willingly and with a smile.

"Are you being treated well here?" Miss Finlay must have asked for at least the third time.

"*Mais oui*," the girl replied. "It's the best place to work. I consider myself lucky to have found this position."

"She does seem content working here." Miss Finlay wore a puzzled frown on her face. "I wonder why."

"Are you referring to the gossip that this *château* has a dungeon where the vicomte locks up his servants at night?" Philippe couldn't help teasing her.

Miss Finlay leaned forward, her eyes wide. "You've heard the stories too?"

Ciel! She really believed those rumours to be true? He decided to test her. "Oh yes. The vicomte's dungeons are notorious. Many a soul has disappeared in them, never to be seen again. A pity Madame Motte forgot to show them to us, for I would have loved to have had a glimpse of this infernal place. Dante is said to have found inspiration here for his epic poem 'Inferno'." He watched her reaction closely.

She laughed uneasily. "That sounds like a bag of moonshine."

"Who knows? There is some truth to every rumour."

"I quite agree," Miss Finlay muttered.

"One thing's for sure, he certainly has a good wine cellar, your vicomte." Philippe swirled a glass of Burgundy and sniffed at it.

"He's not my vicomte," Miss Finlay said, predictably. "And stop smirking."

Philippe chuckled. "It's only because I anticipated your reaction, and I enjoy teasing you. But I see you are not in the mood for teasing. Here, try this cheese. It is excellent." He placed a slice of creamy cheese on her plate, but she just stared at it, lost in thought.

"A penny for your thoughts?"

"I've been having all manner of strange thoughts, indeed." She popped the piece of brie into her mouth, chewed, swallowed, and licked her fingers. "Pray, what do you think is the purpose of marriage? Aside from the obvious financial considerations behind it, of course."

For a moment, he was taken aback. Then he said, "To have a partner in life, so it's not so lonely."

"A sweet thing to say, but quite wrong." She looked at him from under her eyelashes. "Are you a secret romantic, Mr Brown?"

He folded his arms. "Then tell me what the purpose of marriage is, oh wise one?"

"Simple. It is procreation."

He cleared his throat and looked away. "Well, that too."

"No. Only that. Especially for people of our status. The

sole purpose is to produce an heir. To continue the family line. There is no other purpose, romantic or otherwise. And for that purpose, women are needed."

"Must we discuss this in such, er, frank terms?" he muttered. "Over the supper table, too?"

"Yes, we must. Because, you see, in my case, it simply won't work."

He set down his wineglass, fascinated. "It won't?"

She shook her head firmly. "No."

"I am terrified to ask, but I must." He leaned forward. "Why not?" he whispered.

Mellie also leaned forward and whispered. "Because Monsieur le Vicomte has overlooked something very important."

"I'm beginning to feel awfully apprehensive to learn what that might be," he whispered back.

"Why are we whispering? This is neither a secret nor something to be embarrassed about." She took a big breath. "You see, the thing is this." She twisted the fork between her fingers. "What the vicomte doesn't know is that we Finlays only produce girls. Generations and generations of girls. Not a single son. Father only got his title because a distant relative passed away and there was, you guessed it, no immediate male heir in his family. But it's funny, isn't it? Chances are excellent that I will have only daughters, thereby becoming responsible for the death of the Fouquet de Lacasse family line. I must admit, I'm enjoying the look on your face." She sat back, as if satisfied to have left him speechless.

"I must say, there is nothing wrong with girls, is there?" He thought for a moment before adding, "Come to think of it, I daresay I could live with only having daughters." He was beginning to warm up to the subject. "In fact, the more

I think about it, the more I like the idea. I suppose one could find some other chap in the family to carry on the blasted family name—" he interrupted himself as Mellie beamed at him.

"Yes, you would say something like that, because you are a nice, kind man. I like you very much, you know?"

He gave her a quick look. "You do?"

"Yes. I wouldn't mind marrying you at all." She reached for her wineglass and took a sip, entirely unaware that he was sitting there speechless, feeling as if he had just been struck by Zeus's lightning bolt.

"I think I misheard," he said when he had recovered. "Would you care to repeat what you just said?"

"That part where it was typical of you to say something nice about my shocking confession about only having girls?"

"No, that part that came after."

She thought. "Oh! You mean how I wouldn't mind marrying you." She plucked a grape from the fruit bowl. "Although I suppose there must be dozens of girls who would say the same. I wouldn't be surprised if you were quite the catch on the marriage mart, Mr Brown."

He'd forgotten how many times she'd astonished him with her assertions throughout the course of this extraordinary conversation. This had to be at least the tenth time.

"To sum up," she continued. "It is a fact I'll fail miserably in producing a son. I shall have to give birth to girl after girl after girl, say nine or ten of them, until I die in childbirth." She pursed her lips. "Unless he throws me into the dungeon first, which is likely, given my recalcitrant character. So, you see, I will probably either end up locked up in a dungeon or die giving birth." She thought. "Probably both." She popped the grape into her mouth and chewed it.

Philippe choked on his wine. "What an utterly depressing prospect," he managed to say after he had finished coughing. "Is this really what you think is in store for you?"

"Yes, it is the fate that awaits me. And another reason why I don't want to get married." She picked up another grape but stared at it morosely instead of eating it.

He pushed his plate away. "I have thoroughly lost my appetite. That was the most depressing discourse of marriage and childbearing I have ever heard. Be that as it may, you have thoroughly convinced me. You must not marry this vicomte. In fact, you must not marry at all. Ever. Now, can we please change the subject?"

"You see, this is what I keep saying. I would rather not die, and I would rather remain your nephew or be your valet." She looked at him hopefully. "Now that we have seen Charbonneau, shall we travel to Italy next?"

"You know we cannot," he said gently.

Miss Finlay dropped her head. "I know." She heaved a sigh. "Mr Brown?"

"What now, imp?"

She hesitated. "I just want you to know that I am honoured to have met you. It makes me happy to know that there are men like you out there. Kind-hearted and gentle and honourable and caring. Not like that horrid, vicious, lecherous rake I am to marry."

"I—what?" The devil? What was that all about?

"I'd lost all faith in men, you know. Including my father." She rose from the table. "But meeting you made me realise that there are still good men out there." She gave him a watery smile.

Philippe stared after her, stunned, as she fled from the room.

THE NEXT MORNING, the storm had indeed passed, and the sky was clear. From here, they would take one of the vicomte's comfortable chaises to Paris. They would no longer have to endure bumpy rides in hired chaises, nor long dusty walks on dangerous roads. Madame Motte herself had offered it, and it never occurred to Mellie to ask why. She wrapped Mellie in a woollen blanket, packed her into the chaise with a basket stuffed with food, and waved them off.

She'd been awkwardly silent ever since the chaise had left the estate. She stared out of the window, deep in thought, chewing on her thumbnail, avoiding any kind of eye contact with Mr Brown.

Once or twice, he cleared his throat and tried to make conversation, but she ignored him.

"One thing has been bothering me," he finally began. "About our conversation yesterday."

She felt the heat rise in her cheeks. "Pray, forget everything I said last night. I said many inappropriate things, and I am truly very embarrassed now. I must have had too much wine. Yes, that's it. It was merely the wine talking." She placed her hands over her cheeks.

"Pity," he murmured to himself, "I did not at all get the impression that you were drunk."

"Yes, I'm very ashamed of myself now, so let's not lose another word over it."

"Very well. I shall not press you further if you'd rather not talk."

Mellie gave him a grateful smile. They rode on in silence, and after a while she fell asleep.

When the chaise pulled into Paris, Mellie awoke. The city was alive with a vibrant energy, echoing with the hustle and bustle of everyday life. Traffic was dense with carriages, one-horse cabriolets, and other vehicles clattering down the narrow, cobbled roads. Tall, magnificent mansions with intricate façades and ornamental sculptures lined the streets. People were everywhere, walking on the pavement and the road, oftentimes jumping in between the carriages. There was a din of clattering of hooves and the rolling of wheels, the calls of sweetmeat sellers, street stalls, and performers. There was much mud and dirt in the streets, and the putrid stench. Dear heavens! The mixture of odours from the sewers, slaughterhouses, leather tanners, and fish markets was overpowering.

"Where are we?" Mellie rubbed her eyes sleepily.

"We are just passing the Porte Saint-Denis," said Mr Brown.

The chaise turned into the Rue Saint-Honoré and stopped in front of a stately stone townhouse that her mother had rented for the duration of their stay in Paris.

"Where will you be staying?" Mellie asked in a quiet voice.

He thought for a moment before answering, "Some hotel in the Faubourg St Germain, I suppose. I haven't decided where yet."

"Wouldn't it be better for you to rent a private room somewhere?" Mellie asked.

"I'm not staying in Paris that long," was his cryptic reply.

"I see." She felt a heaviness sink in her heart. She mustered all her courage before asking, "Could we not see some sights together? This is my first time in Paris. I would love to see the gardens of the Tuileries, and Notre Dame, and the bridges over the Seine..." Her voice trailed off as he did not answer.

Mellie was about to ask how long exactly he planned to stay, when Mr Brown suddenly said, "Here's your aunt. I informed her we'd arrive today."

Indeed, the door to the house opened and Aunt Wilma rushed out, followed by the butler and a pair of footmen.

Aunt Wilma clapped her hands together over her head when she saw Mellie. "Faith, child, what is the meaning of this? Have you been traipsing about France in this inappropriate outfit?"

Mellie had completely forgotten that she was still wearing boy's clothes. "I thought it'd be more prudent to be a lad than a woman when travelling alone," she explained after she'd hugged her aunt.

"Don't let your mother see you like this. She will swoon again, and we can't have that. Mr Brown," she turned to him with narrowed eyes, "you allowed her to do this?"

"I thought it was safer, aye. Both in terms of physical safety and regarding her reputation. Besides, there was no opportunity for us to acquire appropriate female clothing on the road."

Aunt Wilma sniffed. "Well, I must say nothing shocks me anymore when it comes to my niece. I must thank you, Mr Brown, for bringing her here safely here. I was beginning to fear the worst. Mind you, the worst has already happened since the child has missed her wedding. It is a disaster of immense proportions. I don't even know where to begin. Come, come, child, we must talk. Mr Brown, will you join us for a cup of tea?"

"No, madame, thank you. I shall bid you goodbye here."

Mr Brown turned to Mellie. "Miss Finlay. Your servant." He bowed briefly.

Mellie felt a pang as she realised he was truly leaving. "Will I not see you again, Mr Brown?"

He gave her a lopsided smile. "You will be very busy in the coming days, I expect, and I must resume my travels."

Panic rushed through her. "Oh, but we must thank you properly; don't you agree, Aunt Wilma? Mr Brown went out of his way to save me from being stranded on the road." She turned to him. "Mr Brown, you can't just leave like that. How about some tea tomorrow, then? Can't you come and call on us?"

He hesitated. "It would be my pleasure; however, I am not at all certain it will be possible."

Mellie felt a rush of tears well up in her eyes. "Is that it, then? Do I bid you farewell? W-will I never see you again, then, Mr Brown?"

He took her hand in his and squeezed it gently. "I am certain our paths will cross again someday."

With a nod, he turned and climbed back into the chaise.

"Someday?" she whispered. That word did nothing to console the feeling of emptiness that had taken hold of her heart. She watched as the chaise took off and disappeared down the road.

It took all her willpower not to burst into tears.

CHAPTER 9

Her mother entered the drawing room with her sister, Violet. Violet was the opposite of Mellie in terms of appearance and character. Where Mellie was tall and slender with vibrant dark hair and expressive eyes, her younger sister Violet was small and delicate, with a fair complexion, light blonde ringlets, and blue-green eyes. She looked like a fragile porcelain doll, but this was deceptive, for Violet had a strong personality and a will stronger than steel.

"Mellie!" She immediately rushed forward and hugged her. "What a relief to see you arrive safely. I never doubted you'd make it, but Mama already saw you kidnapped or lying dead in a ditch."

Their mother, Lady Culkirk, was an exceptionally beautiful woman. Her dark hair was still untouched by grey, and her figure was youthful and slim. People said that Mellie inherited her beauty from her, for she had the same complexion and graceful figure.

She sailed into the room, paused dramatically at the

door, and then squealed. "My daughter! My child! You have finally arrived." She kissed Mellie on both cheeks.

"Mama!"

"But, child, child! Look at you!" She held her daughter at an arm's length as she took in Mellie's boyish appearance with a horrified expression on her face. "Do not tell me you travelled through all of France in that outfit!"

"I think she looks splendid, Mama." Violet giggled. "You make a dashing lad, Mel. Oh, what adventures you must have had!"

"Adventures! Aye, let's talk about all the adventures and troubles we've had in the last few days. The wedding! The vicomte! A disaster." Lady Culkirk fanned herself with a silk fan. "You can't imagine how put out we were when we learned of your delay, and then you'd gone missing! Oh, my nerves." She sank into a fauteuil.

"Was the vicomte very angry when the wedding was called off?" Mellie asked in a low voice.

"Truth be told, we don't know, as we have to meet him, still," Aunt Wilma put in. "I notified him immediately upon my arrival in Paris. I emphasised that you are not to blame. Maybe it is for the best, even. Now that the wedding has been postponed, you'll have some time to recuperate and adapt to society life."

"Postponed?" Mellie interjected. "What do you mean? It isn't called off?"

"Called off!" Her mother sat up. "What are you saying? Certainly not! We would never cancel the grandest wedding of the Season."

"Are you saying after all this, he still wants to marry me?"

"Of course he does. What an odd thing to say, Melinda," her mother put in. "Admittedly, it must have taken an enormous amount of organisation to postpone the wedding, what with reorganising all the social events and parties that are to follow. And Wilma is right. Maybe it was for the best, for now there is plenty of time to introduce you to society and to put the finishing touches on your wardrobe. In fact, I much prefer it this way."

Mellie fell back in her chair and stifled a groan. Postponed!

"You shall have a December wedding now. It will be all the crack! I have already sent a footman to notify the vicomte of your arrival, and he will, no doubt, make an appearance soon. You are finally to receive your *corbeille*, which the vicomte insisted on giving you personally. I am certain your wedding basket will be filled with the most exquisite things: jewels, fans, and shawls, and more."

"He is coming here now?" That would be a disaster.

"Indeed. You must be quick. Get out of those awful clothes, have a sponge bath, and get ready! Fie, your hair!" Her mother lifted a strand of her hair with two fingers. "It needs to be properly coiffed. That alone takes several hours. You must look your best when he calls, especially now, being the root of all this fiasco."

Her mother took her by the hand and dragged her out of the room.

Mellie did as her mother bid her. The maid sponged her down in a bath and helped her change into a light green *robe a l'anglaise,* which was parted in the front to reveal a pretty petticoat, then brushed, pomaded, and powdered her hair.

Just as the maid tied a sash around her head, Violet burst into the room. "He's arrived, Mellie. He's waiting for you downstairs in the blue drawing room. Mama says you must make haste."

Mellie felt a sickening punch in her stomach.

Both maids were now tucking and pulling at her dress, pinning on the stomacher, tying all the ribbons, and then unanimously declaring that she looked "*très belle*".

Violet took her hand and pulled her down the stairs. Voices emerged from the blue drawing room below. One of them was distinctly masculine. Mellie stopped halfway down the stairs.

Violet looked at her questioningly. "What's the matter? You've gone pale."

"I can't, Vi." Her breathing was rapid and shallow. Dizziness overcame her. "I really can't. Please. You must help me."

"What do you want me to do?"

"Make me disappear. Fast!"

Violet thought quickly, then she opened a small door in the wall and pushed Mellie inside. "Wait here."

It led to the servants' stairs. Mellie leaned against the wall and tried to control her breathing. After a while, Violet arrived with coats and bonnets.

"Mama will kill me," she muttered as she wrapped the cloak around Mellie and tied the bonnet under her chin. She threw on a cloak herself. "Right after she kills you. But as far as I'm concerned, if the vicomte has been waiting for you all this time, it won't hurt him to wait a wee bit longer. If we follow these stairs down, we'll end up in the kitchen, and we can use the back door. Let's take a walk."

Mellie squeezed Violet's arm. "You're an angel."

"I know. Off we go. And let's not think about the fuss when they discover you've disappeared again."

THE GIRLS TOOK a walk in the Jardins des Tuileries, not far from their residence. The whole park was laid out in symmetric squares with boxwood hedges and cypress trees, and statues in between now dormant flower beds. In the springtime, the garden would be awash with colour when the pink magnolia trees, the white cherry blossoms, yellow daffodils, and red tulips bloomed. They walked down the main alley, starting at the Palais des Tuileries, toward the Place de Louis XV. Since the weather was pleasant, the park was filled with people strolling about: couples, macaronis, ladies with parasols, and children hitting hoops with sticks.

Violet pulled Mellie onto a nearby bench.

"There," she said. "Now tell me why you ran away from your bridegroom and why your face is identical to that of Persephone when she realises she's stuck in the under-world." Violet pointed at a statue next to them of Perse-phone with an expression of dismay and horror on her face.

"I don't know what to do, Vi," Mellie burst out. Then she told her the whole story.

When she finished, Violet shook her head. "You can't keep running from him forever. I daresay you would feel so much better if you finally faced him."

Mellie hung her head. How was it that her sister, five years her junior, appeared to be more mature than she was? "You are probably right. I am being silly, aren't I?"

"If you really can't bear the idea of marrying him, and I don't blame you in the least, I'd be honest about your feel-ings. Go to him. Talk to him. Tell him you want to call it off."

"All hell will break loose if I do that."

"Yes, it might. But what is the alternative? Keep running away from him? Wait until the eleventh hour and desert him at the moment of vows?"

Mellie twisted the silk between her fingers and crumpled it. "I dread having to face him."

"I understand that. It's not pleasant. But consider the alternative: a lifetime of being married to someone you loathe." Violet shook her head. "I know we're expected to accept that fate, but I certainly won't when it's my turn." She threw her head back.

"The thing is, Vi, if I call off the wedding, it will cause such a scandal. It will destroy not only my reputation, but yours as well. And Mama's and Aunt Wilma's. We'll become social pariahs."

Violet shrugged. "I daresay I'd survive."

"No, you won't. You know you won't. You've been looking forward to your Season all these years. If I don't marry him, you won't even have a Season." Mellie rested her head against her sister's shoulder. "But if I do marry him, your marriage prospects will improve drastically. All doors will open, and your hand will be in great demand."

"I don't want you to sacrifice yourself for me, Mel," Violet said. "Don't do it."

An idea occurred to Mellie. "Vi? How many hôtels are there in the Faubourg St Germain? You've been here in Paris longer than me, so you would know."

"I'm not certain. Why?"

"Where would a gentleman on the Grand Tour stay?"

Violet thought. "The Hôtel Imperial, maybe? Or the Anjou? Across the Seine. It's not far from here."

Mellie tugged her sleeve. "Then, let's go."

"Why?" Violet resisted. "Never say. Do you want to find this Mr Brown? Mellie." She came to a halt and grabbed her by both arms. "This is folly. You haven't fallen in love with him, have you?"

Mellie hesitated a moment too long, then looked away. "Of c-course not."

"Then why do you want to visit him when your future husband is waiting for you at home?" Violet persisted.

Because she missed him. Because she wanted to see him again. Because her heart ached just thinking about him. Because the thought that she would never see him again made her fall into a bottomless pit of despair.

"I just...need to talk to him. I forgot to tell him something."

"But, Mellie, even I know we can't just walk into the Imperial and ask for your Mr Brown. It is not only improper, it's positively indecent. If word gets out and Mama and Aunt Wilma find out——"

"Or the vicomte——" The girls' eyes met.

"You'd be ruined for life."

"He must not find out, then. I could say that he is our tutor and that we have a message to deliver. I just want to talk to him for ten minutes, Vi. Please?"

Violet stared at her for one moment. "Very well. But I hope I don't ride you deeper into trouble by helping you."

They took one of the *fiacres* that was waiting at the entrance to the park. They drove over the Pont Neuf, a laborious affair as the bridge was clogged with people and vehicles, performers and stalls.

"We could've been there faster if we had walked," Mellie grumbled.

"Faster, perhaps, but the dirt and stench of the quays would annihilate us before we reached the place," Violet replied, pulling out a scented handkerchief and pressing it to her nose.

The coach took them to both the Anjou and the Imperial, but neither hôtel had any Mr Brown registered amongst its guests.

"*Je suis désolé*, but there is no Monsieur Brown, mademoiselle," a concierge told them. "May I ask who is enquiring?"

"Mademoiselle Melinda Finlay—Ow!" Mellie winced as Violet elbowed her in her ribs. Violet threw a "*Merci beaucoup!*" at the concierge and dragged Mellie away.

"Have you lost your mind entirely?" she hissed as she shoved her out the door to the *fiacre* outside. "Have you gone completely mad? You can't give him your name!"

Mellie shrugged. "Why not?"

"Really, Mellie. Have you been living under a stone? Your name appeared in the *Gazette* only this morning, along with all the other scandal sheets! Mademoiselle Melinda Finlay is well known! Gentlemen are already placing wagers on whether *la belle fiancée anglaise du vicomte* will desert him at the altar a third time."

Mellie regarded her sister with an open mouth.

"You know it wasn't my fault!" Except, of course, it was in a way. "The first time the wedding had to be delayed because I was ill."

Violet lifted an ironic eyebrow. "We both know it was a ruse."

Well. She'd pretended to have the smallpox then, but no one knew, did they? Other than Mama, Violet, and Aunt Wilma.

"Then, we were delayed in Dover, and I missed the *coche*." Deliberately.

Violet waved it away. "I know, of course, that it was not your fault this time. But everyone else prefers a different version of the story. They are saying that the vicomte's beautiful little English bride is leading him a merry dance.

94

Whether intentional or not, you made a laughingstock out of him. You humiliated him quite thoroughly. All eyes are on you to see what you might do next. Part of me cannot help but feel somewhat sorry for your bridegroom, dreadful as he is."

Mellie swallowed. She hadn't thought of that. "Good thing I avoided him today, then." But for how long could she keep doing that?

"As I said earlier, you should finally face him, Mellie."

Once again, her sister proved that she was the wiser of the two.

"I really would like to find Mr Brown." Mellie hung her head.

"He could have taken a room in any other hôtel." Violet put her arm around her shoulders. "Or even a private room. It would be foolish to visit all the hôtels in Paris to find him. You know it's not the thing to do. Maybe he will call or write. Why not wait?"

Mellie's spirits were dampened, and she sighed. "You are right. Let us return home and face the consequences."

To Mellie's great relief, there was no chaise waiting outside of their home, which meant that the vicomte had already left.

"Missed him. What a shame." She sighed with relief.

They were greeted by her aunt, who was pacing the foyer.

"Where have you been? Your bridegroom waited for you for a good hour and then left. He was very displeased. Your mother is in hysterics in the drawing room."

"Violet and I took a walk in the Jardins des Tuileries." Mellie conveniently forgot to mention their excursion to the hôtels.

"Now? Of all times!"

"I just thought since the weather is nice it would be a good thing to do..." Mellie's voice trailed off.

Her aunt took her hand in hers. "You can't run away from him forever, child," she said, echoing Violet's statement.

Mellie hung her head. "I know."

But she very much wanted to run for a little while longer.

CHAPTER 10

The next morning, Aunt Wilma and her mother considered calling on the vicomte.

"You must offer your apologies, Melinda," her mother had insisted.

So, she was dressed in one of her finest silk gowns, her hair pomaded and powdered, beribboned and bedecked in jewellery, ready to be presented to her future husband like a tidy gift parcel. In the same manner of thought, Lady Culkirk had ordered a huge basket of fruit, which they would bring along as a gift.

"If only we could offer him a pineapple!" Aunt Wilma exclaimed. "To mollify him somewhat. Alas, they are impossible to obtain. Pineapples cost a fortune, and I would have had to sell both your mother's and my diamond neck-laces to buy a single small one." She sniffed. "Though I have to say, it might make more sense to just hand over the diamonds than the fruit, which has the propensity to rot within a week."

Mellie had a cold hard lump lodged in her stomach when she thought of the vicomte.

"You must tell him you are sorry, that you didn't know he was coming to call on you, and that you had decided to set out to go shopping with Violet to buy some items for the wedding," her mother instructed her. "It was unfortunate that he happened to come calling just when you were out."

Just before they were about to enter the chaise, a footman arrived with the news that the vicomte was out of town and expected to return within a few days.

"Thank the heavens," Mellie breathed. She felt as if she had narrowly escaped the executioner's axe.

"He's a very busy man, no doubt," her mother remarked. "No matter. There will be other opportunities for you to meet him. Did I tell you that the first time I saw your father was *after* we were married?"

"At least a hundred times," Mellie muttered under her breath.

"I could hardly see him with the veil covering my eyes, and the room was dim because there was a storm raging outside," her mother continued, lost in reminiscence. "It was only at the wedding breakfast that I truly saw Culkirk's face for the first time." She paused, fiddling with the tip of her shawl. "He was so handsome, and I fell in love instantly. I am certain it will be the same for you."

"Yes, yes, you were lucky that Culkirk was quite dashing in his younger days," Aunt Wilma interjected with a hint of sarcasm. "That was, of course, before my brother developed a bald head and a paunch."

Settling into an armchair, Mellie puckered her forehead to a frown. "I will never understand Papa. What did he find so appealing about the vicomte that he arranged a marriage between us?"

"He was good friends with his father, Mellie," her mother explained patiently. "They both went on the Grand

Tour together. I daresay that formed a bond between them that lasted a lifetime, including an agreement that their children would one day marry. I don't know why you dislike him so. The vicomte is quite courteous, a perfect gentleman." She added hastily, "No doubt you will see for yourself once he has returned, and he comes calling again. For now, let us not waste any more time, for we must prepare for a *soiree* at the British Ambassador's residence tonight. It will be your first official social event in Paris, Melinda, and we must ensure your appearance there will be perfect."

To HER SURPRISE, she enjoyed the soiree at the British Ambassador's residence in the rue Jacob. It was a glamorous evening, and Mellie admired the fashion of the guests who attended. The ladies were dressed in the latest pastel-coloured gowns with intricate laces, feathers, ribbons, and low necklines, and the gentlemen sported elaborately embroidered waistcoats and powdered wigs.

She herself wore a pink silk gown with puffed and ruffled sleeves, and a fine shawl draped over her bare shoulders. The tight-fitted bodice was adorned with intricate embroidery and accentuated her waist, from which the multi-layered skirt flared out over wide panniers. Her hair was powdered, and two long curls were draped over her pale *décolleté*.

When she'd come down the stairs, her aunt had taken one look at her, sniffed, and said, "You'll do."

"She's a flower." Her mother had plucked at her shawl and dress and inserted a rose in her hair. "There. You will be the belle of the evening."

For Violet, who was allowed to attend as well, it was her first social event. She was dressed in a pale blue *robe à l'anglaise*, with gently powdered hair.

The connecting doors of several smaller rooms were opened to form a suite of adjoining rooms. Champagne flowed freely, and trays of delectable canapés and petit fours were presented by attentive footmen. Lord Stormont, the ambassador, was a pleasant man who regaled his guests with amusing stories about the queen from his time as ambassador in Vienna. "You will find Versailles a most splendid place," he told Mellie. "Architecturally, it is a masterpiece rivalled only by Schönbrunn Palace in Vienna. Alas, that is the only laudable aspect of the place, for it smells worse than the stables." There was a twinkle in his eye as he said this.

"You don't say!" Her mother's eyes widened in horror.

"Indeed, alas, indeed. The noxious odour of the place has caused many a lady with delicate constitution to faint. I take it you have not been to court?"

"Not yet. My daughter is to have her formal presentation after the wedding."

"Ah!" Lord Stormont raised his champagne coupe. "So you are. It is my understanding you are to be congratulated on your forthcoming wedding, Miss Finlay. Rumour has it that your path to the altar has been fraught with certain, er, complications. But surely, we are to expect a happy ending?"

Mellie smiled painfully.

Her mother replied instead. "You are too gracious, my lord."

"Allow me to be presumptuous and offer you a piece of advice from one who has navigated the matrimonial waters." His voice took on a confidential tone. "No matter what they say, do not marry him unless you love him. I have had the extraordinary fortune of being married to the love of my life. I tell you, there is no greater joy. Regrettably, she was taken from this world eight years ago." A shadow of sorrow briefly crossed his face.

"My heartfelt condolences on the loss of your wife." Mellie looked at him with sympathy and added, "Thank you for your words of wisdom, my lord. I shall take them to heart."

"Oh!" her mother exclaimed. "I did not know you were a romantic, my lord. You must have loved her dearly."

"In all likelihood, I am the biggest romantic in all of Paris. Thus speaks an Englishman." He laughed.

Mellie's mother fluttered with her fan. "I am certain you too, Melinda, will grow to love your husband. But how unfortunate that the vicomte could not attend tonight. They say he has a most pressing trip out of town. Such a busy man!"

"Speaking of the devil." Lord Stormont raised his eyebrow. "It appears you must have been misinformed, my lady. Is that not him? He is entering the salon as we speak." He gestured at the door.

Indeed, heads turned, and a general murmuring filled the room.

Mellie's heart dropped into her shoes. She dragged her eyes up with great physical effort.

A creature in grey and silver posed by the entrance, a snuffbox in one hand, a silk handkerchief in the other. He wore tight knee breeches and silver buckled shoes with high red heels. His full-skirted dark grey coat and waistcoat were lavishly embroidered with silver, the edges trimmed with a pattern of tulips and roses. Several pink tulips were tucked into the top buttonhole of his coat. The finest Brussels lace spilled over his wrists.

His wig was a towering, powdered toupee with a triple layer of side-rolls and tied in the back with ribbons.

But it was his face that made Mellie blink. It was a thick mask of alabaster white, with two red spots, rouged lips, and kohl-rimmed eyes, with eyelashes a girl would die for. A black, heart-shaped beauty patch adorned his cheekbone.

He looked simultaneously effeminate and masculine; ridiculous and beautiful, and one could not help but gape and admire him.

"Good Lord! He looks like a macaroni of the first order," exclaimed a gentleman who was standing next to them.

"Fouquet de Lacasse," the man next to her informed his English companion. "Not to be underestimated. He looks like a ninnyhammer and entirely incapable of putting two and two together, but don't be fooled. His name is feared. Even though his family is of the lower nobility, he's the Queen's favourite and wields enormous power at court. One hears he even advises her on fashion and *maquillage*. It is judicious to be on his good side."

"Indeed?" The man next to him raised his quizzing glass. "I may need an introduction."

The crowd parted before him as the extravagant vision strolled languorously through the room.

"He's coming right at you." Her mother increased the speed at which she was fanning herself. "Remember what we told you. You need to be on your best behaviour now."

Run, darted through Mellie's brain, but her feet had grown roots and refused to move.

She watched with growing alarm as he drew near and paused to briefly greet his host by lifting two fingers. "Stormont."

"Lacasse. A pleasure," Stormont replied with a nod. "We shall converse anon. For now, let me leave you to the company of your charming, prospective in-laws."

Turning to her mother, the vicomte bowed. "Lady Culkirk."

"What an unexpected pleasure to meet you here, Monsieur le Vicomte," her mother chirped. "We expected you to be out of town. But how fortunate that you came, for at long last you can meet our Melinda. Vicomte, I have the great honour of presenting my daughter Mademoiselle Melinda Finlay," she announced with redundant formality. "Melinda, my dear, behold the Vicomte Fouquet de Lacasse, your bridegroom. Curtsy," she hissed, prodding her side.

Mellie did as she was told and bobbed down in an awkward curtsy. "How do you do?" she murmured.

"*Et voilà*. My elusive bride. We meet at last," he said in French and made an ostentatious leg. "After all this time, we are finally formally introduced, an event that is disgracefully overdue, would you not agree?" His soft, languid voice made Mellie's skin crawl.

"It is shamefully tardy, indeed," her mother agreed with a nod, "if one considers how long you have been engaged. Monsieur, is she not beautiful? Tell us, she is at least as beautiful as the queen, if not more, is she not?"

Mellie wished a hole would open in the floor so she could disappear into it.

He curled his lips into a smile.

"Enchanting," he murmured, planting a kiss on the back of her gloved hand. "A beauty, indeed. She'll outshine everyone at court."

She pulled her hand away.

Her mother offered him a radiant smile. "She will indeed." She tapped her fan coquettishly against his arm.

A melodious strain of violins started a minuet.

"If I may have the honour of this dance?" enquired the vicomte.

"Yes, dance, children, dance!" Her mother gave them an encouraging smile.

He extended his hand towards Mellie.

She hesitated. Her mother gave her a discreet nudge.

With a sinking heart, she put her hand in his, allowing herself to be led to the dance floor.

Vicomte Philippe Fouquet de Lacasse was at his wit's end.

She was everything he'd ever wanted in a bride. In the few days they'd spent together, he'd found her to be a vibrant, charming little thing, whose eyes lit up every time they fell on him, making him feel warm and fuzzy, as if whisky was running through his veins. He'd grown to know her as a cheerful, talkative, quick-witted girl who was a delight regardless of whether she was in breeches or in full dress. She was warm-hearted and kind to all people, whether they were peasants, beggars, servants, or random Scottish gentleman tourists, like Mr Brown.

Except to him, the vicomte.

Him, she loathed him with a passion he found baffling.

In his presence, she turned into a cold porcelain doll with a painted smile on her face, hackneyed, polite phrases on her lips, and a look in her eyes that made him cringe. The disgust that had crossed her face as he traversed the room to meet her had left him momentarily speechless.

He was astonished that there was no recognition in her eyes, no realisation that he was the Scottish traveller from Calais. He wasn't wearing as much paint as he usually did at court—the layer of *blanc* paste he applied for that occasion was usually thicker—and he wasn't wearing his most flamboyant court dress, either, but a simpler suit, for the court was still in half-mourning for the previous king, Louis XV.

She was usually so perceptive and intelligent. Why was she so blind when it came to him, both regarding his appearance and personality? Her prejudice towards his person and her refusal to make his acquaintance puzzled him. He'd hoped to clear the air between them by now. That had been his intention when he'd called on them earlier with a huge bouquet of flowers but found her not at home. He'd stayed for an hour, politely conversing with her mother and her aunt, then rose to depart.

Her aunt had followed him out into the hallway. "It was good of you to come straight away," she'd said. "It was the right thing to do. But what are you planning on doing now with Melinda—Mr Brown? And don't look so surprised. Your disguise may fool some people, especially Melinda, but certainly not me." She sniffed.

"I did not don this appearance to maliciously deceive anyone, madame. It is how I usually go about in society. As for not having revealed my identity during the trip, it was because she seemed to trust Mr Brown, and I wanted to keep that trust, given the difficult situation we found ourselves in. So, I deemed it better to leave her in the belief that that was who I really was." Not to mention that he'd been simply too great a coward to reveal the truth then. "This needs to end now, naturally. I came here with the intention of clarifying the situation, but my bride seems uncooperative."

Madame MacKay shook her head. "She's like a skittish colt. Give her more time."

"Time is what we do not have."

She nodded. "Then you must resort to more dramatic measures."

Philippe wondered what that might be.

She grabbed him by the sleeve and pulled him aside. "Must I spell it out, lad? Really, in my day, we were much more straightforward with our affections. The youth of today is sadly lacking in spunk."

"Madame, I have no idea what you are talking about."

"For heaven's sake. Woo her. Court her! Make her fall in love with you. She's already halfway there. It's no use to anyone if she pines for a man who doesn't exist. If you go about this the wrong way, it could kill the budding affection she has developed for Mr Brown and cause her to distrust you. You could lose her altogether."

Indeed, that was also his fear. She already heartily disliked the vicomte. If she discovered that Mr Brown had deceived her, would she despise him as well? What if she found him so repugnant that it would kill any kind of affection, however fleeting, she had for Mr Brown? If he revealed that Mr Brown and the vicomte were one and the same, would the smile of delight she'd had for Mr Brown turn to one of horror?

"You must be crafty. This is what you must do," Madame MacKay said. "You must get her to transfer the affection she has for Mr Brown to the vicomte."

He smiled weakly. "Madame, I will try to do as you say, but I ask one thing of you. Pray, do not reveal my identity to Mademoiselle Finlay just yet. Let her discover it on her own."

She sniffed. "I do not see the point of that at all, but very well. I shall be as silent as the grave."

His plan had been to end the charade, to ease his bride's

worried mind and to reassure her they could look forward to a bright future together. If she still insisted on calling off the wedding after that conversation, then so be it. He believed she wasn't indifferent to him. He wasn't deluding himself, however. What she'd said that evening—that she wouldn't mind marrying Mr Brown—had given him hope, but perhaps that had been a spur-of-the-moment kind of confession borne out of a moment of panic, because she so very much wanted to accompany him to Italy.

He wanted to see her smile at him once more, like that night in Charbonneau, her lips trembling, eyes glowing with trust. He wanted to hear her laugh again, full and rich, and see the impish dance in her eyes. But now, her lips were pressed together, and her eyes were averted.

He gripped her hand tightly as he led her around in a turn. As they danced, they moved through a series of intricate patterns, with small, deliberate steps. But she doggedly refused to meet his eyes.

This wouldn't do. They had to converse. But what did one converse about with a woman who held him in violent dislike? His mind feverishly searched for a topic.

Surprisingly, she spoke first. "I heard you called on us earlier. Alas, I was out. I was," she visibly sought for a reason, "buying silk. Yes. We needed more silk."

"Silk." A flash of irritation shot through him. When he'd called on them, Lady Culkirk had gone off on a lengthy speech on how they'd bought so much silk that they were outfitted for the next three Seasons. "We have enough silk to open our own shop, monsieur!" she'd said.

"Yes," Miss Finlay repeated now. "We ran out of silk for more dresses. I also had to be fitted for a new gown. It took all afternoon."

"Since you were buying silks, it couldn't have been you

traipsing into the Hôtel Imperial looking for a certain Scottish gentleman, could it?" He didn't know what devil prompted him to say that.

She grew pale. "No. It certainly couldn't have been me."

He pulled her close and whispered into her ear, "Liar."

"I'm not lying!" She stumbled over her next step.

"I have it on good authority that the name the lady gave the concierge was Mademoiselle Melinda Finlay. In Paris, gossip spreads like a stain on white linen, swift and ineradicable. Remarkably, it took less than thirty minutes from the moment you entered the hôtel for the rumour to reach me that my elusive fiancée is seeking out her English paramour first thing upon setting foot in Paris." They came to a halt, locked in a mutual gaze.

"This is preposterous!" Her voice trembled with indignation.

"I demand an explanation." His voice sounded colder and more cutting than he'd intended.

"This is absurd. There is no truth to the rumour at all."

"Is it? Yet your actions seem to belie your words. As for that gentleman, it appears I must call him out. It is a matter of honour after all." He watched her closely, gauging her reaction.

She turned ashen. "No. Please don't! I beg of you. There is nothing to explain, as nothing ever happened. I simply wished to visit a friend, that's all."

"Just a friend. Is he?"

"How dare you scrutinise my friends or question my loyalty? You hardly know me yet assume the worst."

"Ah. An excellent turn of phrase. But do I, indeed? Is it not the other way around?"

Tears of anger glistened in her eyes. "How dare you discredit my and Mr Brown's character so vilely, when he has been nothing but kind to me. We owe him a debt of gratitude for having rescued me from a most precarious situation. Whereas you—you are a contemptible libertine of the worst kind."

What nonsense was that?

Realising that the other dancers in the set were staring at them, Philippe pulled her away from the dance floor.

"I see we are attracting attention." He turned to the others. "'Tis a mere lover's quarrel. Pre-wedding nerves, no doubt. Pray resume the dance undisturbed by our presence." He made a gesture with one hand.

The people laughed, and the music resumed.

He really hadn't intended to argue with her. He'd meant to draw her out of her shell, curious to hear how she'd defend herself, given some rather serious allegations in the gossip that was spreading in the salons. He cursed himself. It was a terrible idea to have brought this up in public. He must have been momentarily unhinged. But somehow his emotions had taken the upper hand, and he'd forgotten their surroundings, and their conversation had spiralled out of control. Not only had he managed to upset her, but he'd ended up equally furious. Paradoxically, he also felt a desire to gather her into his arms and laugh at the ridiculousness of it all. Because, really, this entire situation was nothing but absurd.

Her face was like thunder as she brushed past him.

Frowning, he followed her back to her aunt, who had been watching the entire interlude with pursed lips.

"Faith! What a scene you are causing! If I didn't have nerves as steel, I would have fainted a hundred times over. Your poor mother certainly has." She gestured to her mother, who lay limp and groaning in a nearby armchair. "Really, children. I understand that an honest conversation is more than overdue, and aye, do address all your misunderstandings. But I beg you, must you do so in the middle of the ambassador's soiree? If your intention was to dispel the latest rumours, you have just achieved the contrary." Pulling him aside, she hissed into his ear, "I said woo her, not quarrel with her!"

"You are right. The fault is entirely mine. It was unforgivable of me to provoke a quarrel." He turned to Miss Finlay and bowed stiffly. "We shall resume our conversation tomorrow." He hadn't meant it to sound threatening.

Miss Finlay nodded at him coldly. "As you wish, monsieur."

CHAPTER 11

Mellie vowed to herself that under no circumstance would she be at home when he called to resume the "conversation" from the previous day. He could wait for her in the salon until the white paint on his face turned blue.

In the meantime, there was only one thing to do to avoid that situation: go shopping.

And what shopping!

Dragging a reluctant Violet with her, she visited every single silk shop in the Rue Saint-Honoré to buy ribbons, silk stockings, gloves, fans, perfumes, and lace. They'd tried on countless straw hats and shoes and rummaged through an entire shelf of fabric bolts.

In the afternoon, Violet rebelled. "No more. I can't go on. My feet hurt. My head hurts. I'm tired, hungry, and thirsty. Let's go home, Mel. Please!"

Mellie took out her watch. "It's not even three in the afternoon. Surely, he will call any minute now. He must not find me at home."

"He's your future husband! You should talk to him!" Violet said in exasperation.

"We did so yesterday, and it was a catastrophe." Mellie shook her head. "He's as idiotic as he looks. He probably can't help it, but I certainly can by avoiding him as much as possible."

"Honestly, Mel, I find that if you ignore his odd appearance, he doesn't seem all that bad if one considers all the stories we heard about him in London. He was quite polite to me; although, admittedly, he was rather cross with you and looked like he'd wanted nothing more than to give you a thorough flogging. But if you think about it, I would be quite put out as well if my betrothed were to run off every time I made an appearance. You *have* behaved badly."

"I know," Mellie said ruefully. "I suppose I owe him an apology. But I find him difficult to talk to." She sighed. "He thinks I have a paramour."

Violet stared at her, mouth agape. "Your Mr Brown?" Then she weighed her head back and forth. "Isn't he right?"

Mellie slapped her arm. "Whose side are you on? His or mine?"

"The rumours have reached him? He knows about you visiting the Hôtel Imperial?"

Mellie grimaced. "He confronted me about it at the soiree. He talked about calling out Mr Brown."

"This is very bad, Mel. Will he call off the wedding?"

Her face brightened. "Do you think he will?"

"Any other man would."

"But alas, he did not say he would."

"He might not, not if he is a man of honour, and I begin to suspect he might be. Do you know what I think?" Violet looked at her earnestly. "He might want to make it work.

I've only talked to him for a few minutes, and I had the impression that he's shy."

Mellie stared at her sister. "Shy! You can't mean it." There hadn't been a hint of shyness about him yesterday when they ended up quarrelling in the middle of the minuet.

"I do mean it. If I were you, I would spend some time getting to know him before you marry him. And for heaven's sake, Mellie! You must put that Mr Brown out of your head. It won't do you any good if you keep hankering after him."

If only it were that simple.

They walked home, a faithful footman trudging along behind them carrying the parcels.

"There you are, children," their mother greeted them. "And just in time, too. Violet, you are to call on Madame Perpignon with Aunt Wilma. She is a distant relative and expecting your visit; while you, Melinda, are to have a lesson with the dancing master, Monsieur Dupont. I'm told you have not yet mastered the three curtsies that you'll need for your formal presentation at court. It is most imperative that you learn them as soon as possible. Then you have an appointment with Madame Aubert, the *marchand de mode*, who must make alterations to your wedding gown. She will also make your *grand habit de cour*. Your court dress will be a magnificent outfit with a long train and the widest panniers imaginable." She indicated with her hands just how wide. "You'll need to practise walking in it, so you don't stumble and fall when you are presented to the king and queen. You must learn to walk as if you were gliding." To illustrate her point, she stretched out her arms and tiptoed along the floor. "The entire court will be watching you closely and comment on every single mistake you make. After the stories that have been circulating about you these days, you must put in extra effort to prove them all false."

Mellie sighed. "So the wedding is to proceed as planned."

"Certainly," her mother said breezily. "I broached the subject with the vicomte last night, and he brushed the talk off as inconsequential. I must say, he is a very understanding man, given your shocking behaviour recently. Visiting the Imperial on your own, indeed! You really ought to know better, child. We have agreed that you two must be seen more in society to dispel these horrible rumours. But first, Monsieur Dupont."

Violet shook her head with pity. "Good luck, sister. I suppose I can count myself very lucky that I am to only visit Madame Perpignon this afternoon." She squeezed Mellie's arm in sympathetic support, kissed her mother on the cheek, and left.

Mellie threw up both arms with a groan. "Do I really have to do all this, Mama?"

"Melinda! Your future husband is a courtier, and it is expected of his wife to not only be well versed in etiquette but also to look the part as a lady of the court. There must be no hint of a scandal in your appearance or behaviour. Do you understand?"

She rolled her eyes. "And what would my function be as a court lady? To pass a towel on to another court lady, who dries the queen's body after she's bathed? Or to carry out the chamber pot on a silver platter after she's done her business? What an honour."

Her mother saw nothing whatsoever wrong with that. "Indeed, Melinda. It is a great honour to serve the queen. There are many women who dream of such a position, but who will never be admitted to the presence of the king or queen. You, on the other hand, have a bright future ahead of you by your husband's side. Go, get changed, child, for Monsieur Dupont will arrive soon."

Mellie felt the black cloud of depression descend upon her. Was this what her life would be like from now on? Her whole day filled with dreary lessons in etiquette, dancing, curtsying, and standing still while a modiste measured her body. Married to a man she despised, she'd have to perform menial, humiliating tasks for a queen who wasn't even her own, in a glamorous court full of intrigue and vice. Would this be her life?

She curled her hands into fists.

After the maid helped her out of her clothes, she sent out the maid to fetch her a pitcher of hot water to wash her face. While the maid was gone, Mellie slipped into Jerome's suit.

She could no longer rely on Violet's help.

She would have to go out alone—to find Mr Brown on her own before it was too late.

This time, Mellie visited the hôtel on the nearby Rue Denis. She found the anonymity of her boy's disguise reassuring, for as a woman she would not be able to walk on the streets alone. No one gave her a second glance. But that ended as soon as she approached the Croix Dorée. There, she could not even pass the hôtel's doorman, who was waiting at the main entrance. When she tried to enter, the burly man in livery stopped her.

"*Hè*, no entry for the likes of you, boy!"

Mellie bristled. The likes of her? She was wearing Jerome's brother's Sunday suit, freshly washed and pressed, if you please. "I have an urgent message for Monsieur Brown. Please let me pass."

"Hand over the message, and I'll give it to him," replied the doorman.

"I must give it to him directly."

"Impossible." He crossed his arms and spread his legs.

"But I really need to get inside, monsieur!" Mellie tried to push past the man, but he grabbed her by the neck of her suit and threw her down the stairs without much ado.

She rolled down the steps and landed in a miserable heap in the street, her nose pressed against a shiny pair of damask shoes with impossibly high red heels, the buckles studded with diamonds.

Her eyes wandered up a pair of powerful thighs in silk stockings, followed by burgundy silk breeches, a full-skirted coat and lavishly embroidered waistcoat, and more diamonds in an immaculately tied cravat. Her horrified gaze met a lidded, ironic one.

A familiar voice drawled, "Well, well, well. What have we here?"

CHAPTER 12

She should have fought. She should have kicked him in the shins and ran.

But Mellie had been too shocked to do either, or to react to the vicomte's order.

"Take him along."

Before she knew what was happening, she found herself once again grabbed by the scruff of the neck and thrown headlong into a chaise. The door slammed shut, and the vehicle set in motion before she could utter a word.

"I'm not used to being accosted so rudely in the street." The vicomte leaned into a shadowy corner, and his soft voice made her skin crawl.

"Where are you taking me?" For an instant she considered tearing the door open and hurling herself onto the road, but the coach was speeding through the streets, and she would surely end up dead if she did so.

"As it happens, my household is in need of more servants. Particularly the kind who polishes shoes. You shall do nicely."

"You—what?" Mellie was momentarily speechless.

"You have soiled my precious shoes," he complained and stretched out a leg to admire his shoe. "They happen to be my favourite."

"But you can't just take me along. It's kidnapping!"

He gave her a level look. "Is it? What a dramatic term. I call it 'payment for transgression.'"

"What transgression? I fell down the stairs because that brute of a doorman pushed me." She rubbed her smarting knees. "It's not my fault if you happened to be standing there at that moment, monsieur. You can't just take me away and make me your servant. It is illegal." Although it probably wasn't. She knew that people like him could do whatever they wanted to the poor devils of the lower classes and get away with it.

He leaned forward. "I cannot?" he asked softly.

"No, you cannot." She tilted her chin at him.

"You have no inkling, *mon enfant,* of the things I can and cannot do. You ought to count yourself lucky that I am offering you such a humane way out."

She quaked inside. "But I have done nothing wrong!"

"You assaulted an aristocrat." He crossed his arms. "Or is it attempted robbery? I daresay both. You had an eye on my beautiful shoe buckles. Yes, they are real diamonds. What more is there to say?"

Her hair stood on end as she stared at him in horror. "I did no such thing!"

"Pray then, if you do not wish to be in my service, would you prefer the alternative?"

"Yes." Anything but spending another minute in his company.

"Very well then." He lowered the window to give instructions to the coachman. "To the Bastille."

She gasped.

He smiled a cold smile. "I'm sure you have heard that people who are thrown into the Bastille never see the light of day. There is also a torture chamber in there, you know. Most people don't survive."

Mellie was too aghast to utter words. He was every bit as terrible as they said in all the stories she'd heard. No, he was worse. Underneath the styled and painted visage, he was a merciless, cold-blooded brute.

What should she do? What a terrible predicament. She would have to reveal who she was and come up with some story to show that it had all been a misunderstanding. After his displeasure the other night at the soiree, she trembled at the thought of how he would react, having caught her red-handed, and in boy's clothes, too. He might throw her into the Bastille anyway after discovering her real identity. At best, he would call off the wedding.

Her spirits rose somewhat.

It was worth a try.

She closed her eyes to gather courage. Then she took a deep breath. "Monsieur le Vicomte. There is something I must tell you."

"Ah, there we are." The chaise slowed.

What? Had they already reached the Bastille?

Before she could form another coherent thought, the chaise door opened and she was ushered outside. The vicomte grabbed her firmly by the arm and dragged her into the dungeon, which smelled—

Delicious.

A warm, comforting whiff of chocolate, vanilla, and cinnamon enfolded her.

Mellie looked around in amazement.

A wiry, elderly gentleman scuttled forward and bowed.

"Monsieur le Vicomte. It is such an honour. Welcome to Stohrer's *Pâtisserie*. How may I serve you?"

Mellie stared open-mouthed at the mouth-watering array of pastries and cakes in the display vitrine. They came in a range of colours, meticulously crafted and beautifully decorated. The walls of the shop were covered in striped wallpaper in pastel blue and green with buttery yellow trim, and huge gilded mirrors. There were small tables with chairs in an adjoining room. It was not only a *pâtisserie* but also a tearoom.

"Stohrer." The vicomte turned to the man who gazed at them in happy expectation. "We will have a sample of everything from here to there." He pointed from one end of the vitrine to the other. "With tea for the boy and coffee for me. And make sure we are undisturbed."

"Of course, Monsieur le Vicomte. I'll see that the entire room is yours." Stohrer bowed.

A hand placed at the small of her back gave her a gentle nudge towards one of the tables in a niche at the back of the tearoom and pushed her into a chair.

"What are we doing here? Why are you doing this?" Mellie demanded.

He pulled the gloves off his fingers one by one. "Your stomach was growling so loudly the entire ride, it was almost deafening. It behoves me to feed you before I have you thrown into the Bastille."

She fidgeted in her chair, avoiding his gaze. Then, her head hanging, she said, "I have a confession to make. I'm not a boy at all. I merely borrowed some boy's clothes." She took a deep breath before adding, "My name is Melinda Finlay."

There was a brief pause, then he clapped slowly. "Well done, Mademoiselle Finlay. I did not expect you to confess so quickly. I daresay it was the mentioning of the Bastille that frightened you?"

Her head shot up. "You knew?"

"My chaise arrived just at the moment you left the house. I had intended to request the pleasure of a promenade with you, since we clearly have matters to discuss, but once more you seemed to have other plans. Seeing that you were in disguise, running through the streets as if the devil personally were after you, I decided to follow you." He watched her closely.

Her shoulders slumped. "Oh." Then she sat up straight. "You trifled with me," she accused him.

"A little. I daresay you deserved it. You have a tendency to flee the moment I make an appearance. It has become a most irksome habit."

Mellie stiffened. "What do you want?"

"We shall talk." The vicomte crossed his legs. "But first, let us eat."

Monsieur Stohrer placed a large silver platter of cakes in front of them.

"*Voilà*. A sample of each: macaron, choux pastry, madeleine, tarte au citron, tarte au fruit, millefeuille, and petit fours, covered with fondant in the colours pink, yellow, green, and blue. But if I may be so bold as to point out, the speciality of the house is the baba." He pointed to a small round cake. "It's my own invention, soaked in wine, garnished with Chantilly cream, and topped with a lovely little cherry. I personally created this masterpiece for King Stanislaus of Poland. It is delectable."

Mellie's mouth watered. She would have loved to sweep the pastries to the ground and walk out of the *pâtisserie* with her nose held high, but she could not ignore the rumbling of her stomach.

She picked up the small silver fork that had been placed in front of her.

"I suppose it won't hurt to try some of this," she muttered.

"Which one would you like, I wonder?" the vicomte said. "This one, I think." He put the tarte au citron on her plate. "I'll have the macaron, and we'll share the famous baba."

"I also want that one." She pointed to a pistachio green petit four with a cherry on top.

"Anything you wish." He placed it on her plate. "Now eat."

She didn't need to be told twice.

"For your information, I don't usually have people thrown into the Bastille," he said conversationally.

Mellie looked up briefly from her petit four. "You don't?"

"No. I have my own dungeons, you know."

She swallowed and nodded. "I have heard of them."

"You really believe that, do you not?"

"What?"

"That I throw people in dungeons. Among all sorts of other unsavoury things about my character." He put his fork down. "Talk to me."

Her brows furrowed in confusion as she replied, "Talk about what, exactly?"

With unexpected bluntness, he confronted her. "You're considering calling off the wedding."

Her eyes shot up to meet his, but his expression revealed nothing of his emotions.

"Don't act so surprised," he continued, his voice measured. "It's not a Herculean task to reach this conclusion given your recent behaviour. Shall we trace the course of events? Our marriage was arranged by our fathers when we were still young. On your eighteenth birthday, I received a missive saying you weren't ready to be wed and preferred to wait until you turned twenty-one. A sensible decision. But when I journeyed to Scotland on your twenty-first birthday for an introduction, you'd disappeared, and then when you were found, you were bedridden with the influenza. Alas, I had to depart without a formal presentation. A year later, business brought me to London, and I learned that coincidentally, you were in town as well. I called. Once more, you were unavailable. Once more, you were indisposed." He lifted his hands. "We recognise a pattern here, do we not?"

Mellie avoided meeting his glance.

"Despite your father's unfortunate demise and our inability to meet, the wedding was to take place in July this year. But then," he spread his hands out on the table as if to study his fingernails, "we were informed you contracted an unexpected bout of the smallpox."

Mellie coughed.

"Of which you miraculously recovered a few weeks later, without a single scar, as far as I can tell." He leaned forward, lifting her chin to study her face. "Flawless," he murmured.

She flushed. "I suppose I was lucky."

"Yes, let us suppose that. After your miraculous recovery, it was agreed that we would defer the wedding to November. Very well. Then it turned out that even that was not to be, due to the unexpected intervention of the elements. You were delayed at Dover, then you missed the *coche*."

"None of that was my fault," Mellie defended herself.

"Indeed. Yet I cannot help but think that you were not

too displeased about missing the wedding. So in total, if we were to calculate, we had two failed meetings in England, two here in Paris, and two official postponements of the wedding. Not to mention all my letters, which remained unanswered. Given all this, it begs the following question: why do you dislike me so much? Is the thought of being married to me so repulsive to you?"

The short and honest answer was a resounding yes. How to put it diplomatically?

"Tell me why," he demanded, seeing her hesitation.

She took a deep breath. "Very well. I shall tell you everything. It isn't just the rumours that I'd heard about you that frightened me. It is because that time in London, at the opera, I saw you seducing a woman."

He stared. "Impossible."

She set her mouth in a stubborn line. "I saw what I saw. I stepped out of my box into the corridor, and I turned and glimpsed into the next box. I saw you with a woman in a very compromising situation. D-doing things to her."

"Doing things?" he echoed.

She made a vague gesture with her hand. "You know."

He crossed his arms and gave her a hard look. "You'll have to be more specific, Mademoiselle Finlay."

She covered her face with both hands and shook her head as she remembered seeing him in the shadowy corner of the box, passionately kissing a lady. She'd only seen his back, but she'd clearly recognised the wig, and the velvet suit with the blue sash. With a gasp, she'd retreated into the corridor, her gloved hand pressed against her mouth. Then, she'd rushed back to her own box and begged her mother to allow her to return home, claiming she felt unwell. That incident had confirmed that all the stories circulating about him must be undoubtedly true.

"Good heavens."

"Yes." Her face flushed.

"Mademoiselle Finlay." He shook his head.

"I abhor infidelity," Mellie declared. "I know it is considered commonplace and the way of the world. I know it is expected of women to look the other way and to accept when their husbands pursue other affections." Her fingernails bit into the palms of her hands as she clenched them into fists. "I cannot be like that. I refuse to be like that. I won't ever be like that."

She shook her head, and her eyes burned with tears.

Her father had been like that.

Her father, whom she had adored.

He had professed to love his wife but had had mistresses his entire life. Her mother—pretty and frivolous —had smiled and dutifully looked the other way.

Mellie would rather die than suffer the same fate as her mother. She'd vowed she would never have a marriage like her parents'.

"Mademoiselle Finlay," the vicomte repeated.

"I don't want to have an unfaithful husband before I even marry. The thought is unbearable to me. So, if you expect me to be a submissive wife who will look the other way while you carry on with your lady paramours, it won't happen. I beg you to call off the wedding. It will do neither of us any good."

"Mademoiselle Finlay," he sighed. "Will you please let me have my say?"

She crossed her arms and looked at him mulishly. "Very well. Speak."

"Thank you. First of all, I don't have any mistresses. Nor do I intend to have any. I abhor infidelity as much as you."

His gaze was fixed on her flushed cheeks.

"Secondly, what you are telling me is the stuff of a sordid romance novel. I don't seduce women, and certainly not in the London opera, for I have never been there."

"Although I must say I do not see why I should even listen—what?"

"I've never been to the opera in London," he repeated patiently. "I simply haven't had the time. My trip to England was short. As I mentioned earlier, I was there strictly on business, only staying a few days. I learned that you were in town, and I called on you. However, as you might recall, you were indisposed that day, either ill or purposely avoiding me. I would have liked to stay longer to await your recovery, but pressing matters required me to return to Paris immediately."

"Oh. But I am certain it was you I saw you at the opera—"

"How can you be so sure it was me, especially since we had never met before?"

That was a valid question. Mellie chewed on her lower lip as she thought about the events that night. She'd been convinced it was him, without a doubt. Why? Her parents had informed her that her betrothed was in London and that she was to expect to hear from him any day. She'd been apprehensive and nervous about the possibility of a chance encounter in town, and her enjoyment of being in the city had been spoiled. Then, that evening, her mother had insisted they attend a performance at the opera, for they were told he was to be there as well.

"Prior to that, Lady Winterhall, who was with us, pointed at the box across from ours, saying, 'Look, there is the vicomte," Mellie recalled.

Lady Winterhall had pointed at an extravagantly dressed man who was talking to a portly gentleman.

"He also wore paint, like you." Her eyes widened as the realisation dawned on her. "Lady Winterhall may have confused you with someone else. Or she may have meant another vicomte."

He arched an eyebrow. "It seems reasonable to conclude that I'm not the only French vicomte in existence who wears paint."

"I suppose not," she whispered. She'd only ever seen his two-dimensional likeness in a miniature portrait that had been given to her. She'd jumped to the wrong conclusion. What a silly, humiliating mistake to make!

He looked at her thoughtfully. "You were all too ready to believe it was me, without even questioning what you saw. I wonder why?"

"I admit I must have been prejudiced due to everything that I'd heard." She swallowed. "It is painful and humbling to admit that I appear to be the sort of person who allows her opinion of people to be influenced by mere hearsay. What an utterly awful thing to do." Mellie squirmed uncomfortably in her chair. "I owe you a sincere apology." Her gaze fixed on the floor in shame.

To her astonishment, he unexpectedly responded, "Some of those rumours do hold a grain of truth."

Mellie's head shot up. "In what sense?"

"The name Fouquet de Lacasse," he began, "instils fear in people because of my grandfather and father. They left behind a formidable legacy. They governed our lands with an absolute iron will that bordered on tyranny, yet it also brought us stability and prosperity. I daresay stories and rumours must have reached the salons in London long before my time. How unfortunate that you were exposed to them." He looked at her steadily. "But you must also know, I am neither like my father nor grandfather."

Mellie wet her lips. "Why should I believe you?"

He smiled. It was odd, for his face was a stiff mask, yet the corner of his rouged lips turned up, as if he were sincerely amused. "I daresay you will discover the truth in your own time." He seemed to be saying it more to himself than to her.

Mellie wondered for a moment what he meant, but he continued, "So much for me. Now to you. Tell me, mademoiselle, why you are roaming about Paris in the guise of a boy. And why, if you please, must it be this," he wrinkled his nose, "horrendous outfit?" He leaned forward to lift her hastily tied cravat with his lorgnette. "If you must wander about as a boy, I beg you, at least do so in more fashionable clothes, with a properly tied cravat."

"These are Jerome's brother's clothes," she began.

He lifted a white hand. "Tell me the story from the beginning."

In halting words, she told him the entire story.

"Very amusing," he said at the end. "And did you find this Monsieur Brown?"

"I have not."

"Pray, in what matter of importance do you need him?"

She hung her head and did not answer for a long time. "Monsieur," she said at last, kneading her hands into the fabric of her coat. "Even if everything I heard about your person is untrue, and you are entirely faultless and have no mistresses, I still cannot marry you, and I must beg you to call off the wedding."

He looked at her silently for a minute before replying, "Would you care to elaborate why?"

She licked her lips. "The reason is that I think—" She took a big breath. "I think—no, I know for a fact—that I have fallen in love with Mr Brown."

CHAPTER 13

The silence in the room was absolute.

She dropped her head. "I know this is an entirely inappropriate and scandalous thing to say," she continued in a low voice. "It is quite horrible, in fact, for a woman to say this to the man she is about to marry." She wiped a tear from her cheek with the back of her hand. "What a hypocrite I am. I berated you for being unfaithful when I am no better. What must you think of me?"

"Mademoiselle Finlay—" he began.

She raised her hand to interrupt him. "You need not say anything at all. I just felt like it had to be said." She tapped one hand on her chest. "It has been building up in here all this time, pressing down on me like a heavy stone threatening to squash my soul, and I felt that if I did not say it, I would surely burst." She gave a low, watery chuckle. "Only I am confessing this to the wrong man. It is very tragic, is it not? On the day I was supposed to be married to one man, I discovered I was in love with another. Oh, don't look at me like that. I shall neither throw myself off the Pont Neuf nor

129

blow my brains out, although both options now sound awfully tempting."

"Mademoiselle Finlay!"

She jumped to her feet, wringing her hands in agony. "I am terribly sorry for embarrassing you, monsieur. You must be feeling quite shocked and upset and angry. You have every right to be. But please do not throw me in the dungeon for being honest. I just think you should know that ultimately this is the reason why I cannot go on with the wedding." She swallowed painfully, then knelt on the floor in front of him. "I beg you, please release me from this commitment. We would be setting ourselves up for great unhappiness otherwise."

He closed his eyes briefly.

Bracing herself for an explosion of wrath, she fixed her eyes on his buckled diamond shoes.

"He doesn't know. Mr Brown, I mean," she babbled. "But I have been trying to find him this entire time because I suppose I want him to know." She sighed again. "Which means that your accusation the other night at the ambassador's soiree was entirely correct. I was chasing after my English paramour after all. I am a despicable person. I am truly sorry." She hung her head, defeated.

He proceeded to regard her with an unreadable expression.

Why wouldn't he say anything? Mellie was burning with mortification. Her knees were starting to ache.

"Surely you can't still want to continue to marry me after all this," she continued, daring to raise her eyes to the lapels of his satin waistcoat.

"It won't do." He got up suddenly. "Let's continue this discussion at home." He took her by the elbow, lifted her up, and led her to the door.

Stohrer came rushing forward. "Monsieur le Vicomte, are you leaving already? But you have not even tried my baba!"

"Another time. I am afraid we have lost all appetite for sweets."

"I shall have it packed up and sent to you, monsieur!" Stohrer called after them.

The vicomte remained silent throughout the entire ride home. The pastries Mellie had consumed earlier sat like cold stones inside of her. Mellie's stomach made a sick lurch every time the chaise jolted over a hole in the street. She shot him furtive glances from her corner in the chaise, unable to read his expression, not daring to say another word. What would happen now? What terrible judgement would be passed on her? Had she done the right thing? What if it had been a grave mistake telling him she loved someone else? How else could she convince him to call off the wedding?

Night had fallen, and the weak streetlamps cast a dim light on the streets. The clatter of the horses' hooves ceased, and the door swung open. Mellie stumbled down the steps of the chaise, caught at the last moment by the vicomte, who grabbed her arm to prevent her from tumbling on the pavement for the second time that day.

She found herself at the entrance to an opulent Renaissance mansion. Its intricate façade was adorned with pillars and sculptures, nestled between tall, softly lit windows.

A line of lackeys stood at the entrance, awaiting their arrival.

Mellie hesitated as she gazed at the imposing house before them. "This isn't my home," she remarked. "Where are we?"

The vicomte stepped up behind her. "This is the Hôtel Lacasse." He held out his hand. "Come."

She stalled. "Why are we here? What are we doing? What are you planning now?"

He took her hand with a firm grip. "You will stay here with your aunt until the wedding. She is already waiting for us."

The wedding? Hadn't he heard a word she'd said earlier? "Stay here? Why?"

"It was a unanimous decision between your mother, your aunt, and me. Yes, it is a breach of etiquette for a couple to stay under the same roof prior to the wedding, but given your penchant for running away in disguise, we deemed it best. We really can't have you wandering around Paris on your own anymore, Mademoiselle Finlay. It won't do."

It was a punishment, she realised. He was going to go through with the wedding no matter what, and then punish her every day for the rest of her life for loving someone else. She could not imagine anything worse.

"So now you think the best solution is to imprison me in your house?" She hated how her voice cracked, hated the tears that threatened to spill over, hated how she was so powerless, so weak.

He gave her a wolfish smile as he bent over her and whispered, "Welcome to the Bastille, Mademoiselle Finlay."

Holding her hand in a firm clasp, he led her into a spacious foyer with a broad marble staircase leading to the upper floors.

The butler stepped forward. "Madame MacKay has already arrived, Monsieur." He did not bat an eyelid at Mellie in her boy's outfit.

"Excellent, Gaubert. See that we are not disturbed."

Mellie struggled in vain to free her hand from his unyielding grip. He led her into a room that looked like a library. Bookshelves lined the walls from floor to ceiling, interrupted only by a row of tall windows on one side and an imposing marble fireplace on the other. Under normal circumstances, she would have been enchanted by this room, but her current state of agitation made her oblivious to its charm.

"Release me." She attempted to wriggle her hand out of his.

Suddenly, he pulled her up against him. "Stop struggling, Max."

It took her a moment to process his words. She stilled. "What...what did you just say?"

He stared down into her face. With a gentle touch, he traced a finger from her temple to her cheek, tenderly tucking a stray curl behind her ear. "Max. Melinda. My little love."

The air between them pulsed and thickened with tension. She stared at him in disbelief.

"It can't be," she whispered. Surely, her eyes must be deceiving her. She was overly tired, possibly dreaming. Yes, that must be it.

She struggled to free herself from his embrace.

He dropped his arms with a sigh. "Let's end this absurd charade. It has got out of hand."

He turned to the gilded mirror that hung over the fireplace and picked off the patches from his cheek. He pulled out a handkerchief, dabbed some scented water from a bottle on it, and rubbed the rouge off his cheeks. Then, with a single motion, he removed the wig. "I should have never started this to begin with. I apologise for my rude behaviour, for a gentleman should never remove his wig in the presence of a lady. But in this case, I am making a point." He tossed the wig onto the sofa and ran both hands through his short brown hair. Then he stepped up to her and cupped her face in his hands, tilting it up. "Look at me."

She stared into his familiar eyes. How could she not have seen it? His eyes had been the same all along. The thick line of kohl around his eyes had deceived her. The paste on his face. Those patches. That ridiculous wig. How could she have been so blind? She lifted her hands to cover her cheeks as the full impact of the revelation hit her. All the blood had drained from her face.

She shook him off and took a step back. "But, but how? But why?" Her legs buckled under her, and she dropped onto the sofa.

"Melinda." He crouched down beside her, a concerned expression on his face.

"Mr Brown," she whispered, "does not exist?"

There was regret in his voice as he said, "I am so very sorry. I borrowed the name from my former tutor."

"But..." Mellie struggled to grasp the implication of what this revelation now meant. "It was all a lie?"

Oh, the humiliation! Oh, the embarrassment! Oh, the things she'd done. The things she said! How could she have been such a fool?

She'd believed Mr Brown to be a genuine, kind man, the kind of man she thought she could be friends with, the kind of man she thought she could fall in love with. She'd been so glad to have met him. She'd yearned for him. She'd scoured all of Paris to be with him.

And now...this?

All the experiences they had shared, the memories they had made together. Had it all been smoke and delusion?

"Not everything, no," he said now, but his voice seemed far away.

In the act of one single moment, it was all revealed to be a sham. By removing his mask and his wig, he'd revealed it all to be fake.

Where did that leave her feelings?

Where did that leave her love?

She gave a hollow laugh. "I believed you. I trusted you. I trusted you so blindly..." And then he'd gone right ahead and betrayed her.

Like her father.

"Foolish, foolish me." Her voice broke. She covered her face with her hands.

"Mademoiselle Finlay. Melinda." He reached up and gently pulled her hands away from her face. "I am sincerely sorry for the deception. I owe you an apology for having deliberately and grossly misled you."

Tears shot into her eyes. "You must have had such a lark with me. Did you enjoy it, playing me for the fool? Did you enjoy playacting and taking advantage of my ignorance?"

He attempted to take her hands again. "You are not a fool. There are few people who know what I look like outside of this mask. They would never recognise me, either. And I derive no pleasure from this deception. Would you believe me when I say that it was never meant to be intentionally malicious, or to hurt you in any way, but on the contrary, merely an attempt to get closer to you? It was badly done. It pains me to admit it was an act of cowardice. Once I started, I did not know how to get out of this cursed masquerade. Especially after you began to develop a fondness for—Mr Brown. *Mon amour*, can you ever forgive me?"

Mellie jerked back as if stung by the endearment. "I am not your love."

"Yes, you are," he insisted. "From the very first moment we met—"

"I don't want to hear it!" she cried, clasping her hands over her ears.

He sighed in resignation. "Very well. But Melinda, about what you said in the *pâtisserie*—"

She drew herself up, pale and proud. "My name is Miss Finlay. And it was a mistake. I take it back. I take back every word I said earlier. And whatever your motivation was for this cruel charade, I do not want to hear it. I do not care who you are, whether you are Mr Brown or the vicomte. Either way, I hate you." With those words, she stumbled to the door and left.

He stared after her, then puffed out his cheeks and exhaled. "*Eh bien,* I suppose one could say that went better than expected," he said into the empty room.

CHAPTER 14

Woo her, Madame MacKay had said.

Win her heart.

Well, he'd made a complete mess of it.

Instead of wooing her, he'd provoked, deceived, scolded, intimidated, and antagonised his bride.

He deserved every ounce of wrath that came his way.

But in his defence, he'd been blisteringly angry. A part of him still bristled at the humiliation he'd suffered when his bride had repeatedly made it clear that she would marry anyone but him. His hair stood on end when he recalled the accusations in the *pâtisserie*. She'd called him a lecherous rake, a philanderer who abused his own servants and seduced random ladies at the opera. She'd attributed a reputation to him that was worse than his father's. He was still horrified beyond words that she'd believed that of him.

In the same breath, she'd said she loved him.

A smile lit up his face.

He would have called off the wedding without hesitation if it hadn't been for the certainty that she'd spoken the truth. Yet he needed confirmation.

137

When they'd chanced upon each other on the stairs the next day, he'd asked her bluntly and without preamble, "Should we call it off? I won't force you into a union that you find repugnant."

But she lifted her head proudly and said, "No." And without further commentary, she'd sailed past him with infinite haughtiness. The relief had been so overwhelming, his knees almost buckled beneath him.

No, he hadn't quite forgiven her for making a laughing-stock of him. He still bristled with the humiliation at the thought that the betting books at the clubs were still open, and more than one friend had enquired when the duel was to take place.

He laughed hollowly at the absurd notion of calling himself out. The better part of him told him to take it with a sense of humour and to shrug it all off. Yet a part of him did not find it funny in the least.

Ah, how complicated all those contradictory emotions were!

It was perfectly understandable that she was confused, angry, and upset with him. She needed time to sort out her feelings, and he would like to give her that time.

But time was exactly what they did not have.

The wedding was only a fortnight away, and if they did not manage to sort out this tangle, they would be starting their married life on the wrong foot.

Was this how it was going to be every morning after they were married? An indifferent bride, sitting like an ice statue at the table, completely immobile, eating morsels like a sparrow?

He suppressed a shudder. How on earth could one woo someone like that?

She was polite to him, all right, and the good news was

that she was still talking to him. In monosyllables. He ought to count himself lucky in that respect.

They sat at a lavishly laid breakfast table. Her aunt, Madame MacKay, usually so voluble with her opinions on all sorts of matters, seemed unusually reticent and focused on eating her eggs and bacon in silence.

He stirred three lumps of sugar into his coffee with concentration.

He took a sip.

He set the cup down again.

The cup rattled against the saucer.

He cleared his throat. "I take it you had a good night's rest, *mon am*–I mean, Mademoiselle Finlay."

"Yes."

She sat up straight, her face as white as a porcelain vase, though he was certain it must have been her natural colour, not paint. There were distinct dark blue rings under her eyes. Her mouth was set in a tight line.

He felt a twinge of sympathy.

His little love. She had probably not slept a wink all night. How could he tell her she was torturing herself needlessly?

"The room is to your liking?" She'd already been given the vicomtesse's room, freshly furnished with furniture from Italy, brocade curtains and lush carpets. As in Charbonneau, he'd personally chosen every single item in the room.

"Yes."

"*Bon, bon.*" He drummed his fingers on the tabletop.

Perhaps the awkwardness was in the language, since they were speaking French? But suddenly switching to English mid-conversation, or non-conversation thereof, would be equally awkward. Why were they speaking

French to begin with? Somehow it was established that when he was the vicomte, they spoke French. When he was Mr Brown, they spoke English.

Would he dare to speak English when he was the vicomte? Would that jolt her out of her reserve and make her thaw a little?

He cast a furtive glance at his bride's impassive face, and all courage left him.

Only the shuffling of the footmen's shoes on the parquet floor could be heard. Not a sound from her, not even a slurp as she drank her tea.

Sacrebleu, what to say now? When in doubt, resort to the weather.

"It appears today it will snow," he said after a quick glance outside. Heavy clouds hung over the city.

"Possibly." She did not even look in his direction.

Well, that was several syllables longer than the previous reply. He ought to congratulate himself.

"I must say, Monsieur le Vicomte," Madame MacKay finally spoke up, lifting her quizzing glass to inspect the table. "Had I known that you already have not one, but two pineapples gracing your dining room table, I would not have put so much effort into finding you one myself. Not that there was any to be found in all of Paris to begin with, as it was an entirely futile endeavour." She sniffed. "Pineapples are horrendously dear and nigh impossible to obtain these days. The best Culkirk could do was to rent one. When he finally found one that was available, it was already half rotten. I remember he displayed it anyway at one of his supper parties. It stank terribly. And here you have two perfectly fresh ones." She shook her head as though in disbelief at such extravagance, pointing to the two pineapples that graced the centrepiece of the table between a huge bouquet of flowers and crystal bowls.

"Indeed," he said more heartily than he'd intended. "I was fortunate to acquire them. But as you rightly point out, two might be an extravagance. Gaubert, serve us one of them."

"*Oui*, monsieur." Without so much as batting an eyelid, Gaubert took one of the pineapples and carried it off to the sideboard, where he proceeded to cut the precious fruit into pieces. He arranged them on small plates and served them.

Madame MacKay stared in horror at the pineapple pieces in front of her. "Good heavens! What a sacrilege. Are you entirely out of your mind? This is like eating gold. No, like diamonds!"

The vicomte speared one of the pieces of pineapple on a little fork and regarded it thoughtfully. "In the end, it is merely fruit," he said and ate it.

He was pleased that this interaction had jolted Mademoiselle Finlay out of her rigid, statuesque posture, as she watched him, open-mouthed, how he consumed with relish all the expensive pieces of pineapple on the plate.

Excellent notion! Woo her with pineapples. Well, if nothing else would do...

"Do try them, Mademoiselle Finlay. They are delicious." He pierced a piece onto her fork and brought it to her mouth.

Petal lips, he noticed, pale pink, soft and utterly kiss-able. How had he come this far and not even attempted to kiss that delectable mouth?

She opened her lips in surprise, and he took advantage of it and popped the pineapple piece into her mouth.

"There. Good?"

She chewed and looked at him wide-eyed. "It's tart, and surprisingly sweet at the same time."

"Like so many things in life." He sat back, supremely pleased with her reaction. "Neither this nor that, neither one nor the other. But a mix of both. That makes things so much more interesting, wouldn't you say?"

She stared at him as if he'd just said something profound. Yes, it was meant to be a reference to himself.

Not Mr Brown. Not the vicomte, but both...

Could she learn to accept that in time?

A drop of pineapple juice slid down her chin. Before she could react, he raised his finger to wipe the juice away. Startled, her own hand shot up. Before she could remove her hand, he took it in his, turned it, and planted a quick kiss on its back. Then he released it.

She flushed and looked away.

Ah. There was some hope yet.

He watched from under his hooded lids as she chewed, finishing the pineapple pieces one by one, deep in thought.

"Your Mr Brown must be rich beyond measure." Madame MacKay, who had not noticed the quick interaction, still had not recovered from the fact that they were eating pineapple.

"Don't call him that," said Mademoiselle Finlay. "I'll never forgive you for not telling me that you knew he wasn't Mr Brown."

"Nonsense, child. Mr Brown, Vicomte, what does it matter what he is called? It is neither here nor there. But I vow, this pineapple is delicious!" Madame MacKay proceeded to savour every bite.

Gaubert entered the room once more, carrying a letter on a silver salver. The elaborate seal on it immediately proclaimed that it came from the court.

Philippe took it, opened it, and perused it. "An invitation to a masked ball at the opera Saturday next. I was not inclined to attend, initially, but it appears my presence is not only expected, but required." He folded up the card and handed it back to Gaubert.

"A masquerade? What sort of nonsensical frippery is that?" Madame MacKay polished her quizzing glass with her napkin.

"It is to be the first ball of its kind to mark the end of the mourning period and the beginning of Carnival," Philippe explained. "I suggest we all attend, together with Lady Culkirk and Miss Violet?"

Madame MacKay's quizzing glass shot up to glare at him. "Out of the question. Violet's hardly out of the schoolroom and only just had her debut. Her first real ball mustn't be a masquerade. I beg you. It is scandalous and improper."

"But, Aunt Wilma, I do not think that society here is as high in the instep as in England." Mademoiselle Finlay put in. "Besides, how fitting for us since none of us seem to be who we say we are. He is Mr Brown, I am Max, and you are apparently my aunt, though I am beginning to have my doubts. Perhaps you've been parading around with a false identity as well. Also, should Violet only go to the boring balls just because she is younger? She deserves to have some fun, too."

"You're talking nonsense as usual, Melinda. Who could I possibly be, apart from myself? The Archbishop of Reims?" Madame MacKay sniffed. "As for Violet, she is a debutante. Think of her reputation. Not, mind you, that either of you seem to put too much stock in that, having done your best to destroy yours with your parading about in boy's clothes and whatnot."

"I beg to differ, Aunt. I don't think anyone ever made the connection between Max and myself."

"Do not underestimate the cleverness of doormen," her aunt said ominously. "Besides, it's not just that. Not to mention everything else regarding this confounded wedding. But let us not rehash the matter." Turning to Philippe, she said, "Do you believe it might be good for either of the girls to attend this masquerade? When neither has been formally presented at court yet?"

He tapped his finger to his lips thoughtfully. "I am to bring Mademoiselle Finlay anyway to introduce her to some people of importance at the ball. There is no such requirement for Mademoiselle Violet. So let us say that whatever Mademoiselle Violet does is her decision. If she chooses to attend, rest assured we shall safeguard her reputation."

Madame MacKay nodded. "Very well, then. Both girls will be in your charge. Melinda, finish your tea, for the dancing master is coming today. You must perfect those curtsies."

Miss Finlay groaned. "Heaven help me."

Philippe suppressed a smile. Yes, they would get there. But slowly.

CHAPTER 15

Mellie tossed and turned in bed that night.
She was simultaneously too hot and too cold; the sheets twisted around her limbs, and she felt suffocated in the room. She got up, opened the window, and breathed in the cool night air. Then she shivered, and her overheated thoughts could find no rest.

She was dreadfully confused.

Her beloved Mr Brown did not exist.

He was a lie, a fabrication, and the pang of grief that shot through her was very real. She'd loved an illusion; of that she was certain.

Mr Brown had vanished and, in his place, the vicomte, the loathsome, despised bridegroom to whom she'd been engaged all these years, revealed himself to be none other than the only man she'd ever fallen in love with.

It made no sense whatsoever.

She no longer knew what to think about the vicomte. He confused her.

The thought of Mr Brown made her heart race and her blood hum louder than a beehive. And when he looked at her like that, like today at the breakfast table, with that incredibly tender, sweet look, as if she were the most precious thing in this world, and when he'd planted that kiss on the back of her hand, all her defences melted and she forgot everything, including her own name, including his.

But wait. The man who had made her feel all that at the breakfast table today had been the vicomte, not Mr Brown.

She had declared her love for him, had she not? But she'd meant Mr Brown, not *him*.

Mellie groaned loudly.

The entire situation was absurd beyond words.

It was enough to drive one mad.

She banged her heated forehead repeatedly against the cool windowpane. "Fool, fool, fool, fool!"

THE FIRST FLURRIES of snow drifted to the ground as they entered the vicomte's chaise that would take them to the opera. Since it was located not far from their townhouse in the Rue Saint-Honoré, they picked up Lady Culkirk and Violet en route. They'd agreed to keep the disguises simple, so all wore dominoes—voluminous, wide-sleeved cloaks over their ballroom dresses, with matching masks.

Mellie's was a light dusty blue and Violet's a delicate pink; Lady Culkirk's a regal red, and Aunt Wilma, who had reluctantly agreed to come, a brilliant forest green. The vicomte's outfit, a striking contrast of cool silver and black, was as splendid and extravagant as ever.

"You must put in more effort in terms of conversing with the vicomte," her mother whispered sharply.

"Remember, tonight is crucial. You must give the impression of being a happily betrothed couple."

Must they? Very well. She could make an effort, if only to appease her mother.

She turned to the vicomte. "Isn't that poison on your face, Monsieur? Lead. I have read about adverse effects of this ingredient in cosmetics. It is said to cause rotting teeth, hair loss, pox marks on the skin, poisoning, and ultimately, death."

"Goodness, child, can't you think of a more uplifting topic? We are on the way to a ball, if I may remind you," her mother scolded her. "It is meant to be a cheerful event."

"But it is true, Mama. Don't you remember? I seem to recall a lady back in England who was said to have died of lead poisoning from her excessive use of lead-laced cosmetics."

"Faith, the child is entirely right," Aunt Wilma put in. "The woman died shortly after her nuptials. What was her name again? It eludes me. Ah, I remember, it was the Countess of Coventry."

The vicomte chuckled. "Why do I have the ominous feeling that you wish for me to befall a similar fate?"

"I am merely pointing out a possible negative side effect of using too much *blanc* and *rouge*. Of course you can apply to your face whatever you want, otherwise," Mellie replied sweetly.

"You do not approve of my use of cosmetics," he observed.

She shrugged one shoulder.

He smiled. "The earlier recipes did indeed contain lead in the powder," he admitted. "I suspect that English cosmetics are much inferior to French ones, so I'm not surprised that it would cause poisoning. However, the recipe I use is homemade and consists of chalk and starch and a pinch of bismuth, which is entirely nontoxic. Not to mention my own secret ingredient, which is, among other things, ground pearls."

"You mean real pearls?" Mellie asked.

"Indeed."

"It appears the man does not know what to do with his wealth," Aunt Wilma commented, shaking her head. "When he does not eat items more precious than gold, like that pineapple, he grinds his pearls to dust and smears them on his face."

"I am happy to share some of my precious powder with you, madame," he said with a grin. "I only allow the queen to use it."

"Oh, do you?" Mellie's mother chimed in. "Then you must share it with me as well. And with Melinda, of course."

"Naturally, madame." He turned to Mellie and lifted her chin with one finger to study her face. "Although, *mon amou* —I mean, *ma chère*. You do not need paste. Your face is naturally pale. Too pale, in fact."

Her pallor was no doubt due to her sleepless nights.

His finger gently brushed her cheek.

Why did such a light touch trigger such confusion in her?

Was he flirting with her? It certainly seemed that way.

Mellie hardly knew where to look. Fortunately, she did not have to reply, because just in that moment, the chaise pulled up in front of the Palais Royal, which housed the Théâtre de l'Opéra.

The masked ball was in full swing.

The Grand Salle of the Opera had been transformed into an immense ballroom. Mellie gazed in amazement at the spectacle before her. The boxes and loges, adorned with gold and rich ornaments, reflected the light from dozens of glittering chandeliers. The ballroom floor teemed with lavishly costumed guests, from allegorical figures to whimsical animals, all moving to the harmonious strains of the minuet. Mellie paused to admire the dancers as they glided across the floor.

"What a crush," Lady Culkirk remarked. "We must be careful not to lose each other. Violet, hold my arm."

Mellie's hand rested on the vicomte's arm, who skilfully guided her through the throng.

A jostle from the crowd caused her to drop her fan. Letting go of the vicomte's arm, she bent to pick it up.

That single moment of distraction caused her to lose her party as they vanished into the swirling crowd. She thought she saw the vicomte's plumed headwear in the crowd and followed it, only to discover it was someone else.

She knew they were heading for his private box, but where was it? Her eyes swept around, but there were hundreds of loges arranged in a semicircle from the ground up.

Filled with a sense of disorientation, she turned and stepped back, inadvertently colliding with a lady dressed in a resplendent silver-white domino.

"Please accept my apologies," Mellie offered courteously, then stared in fascination at the lady's extravagant coiffure. She had never seen anything like it. A white, powdered wig stretched at least thirty-five inches from her forehead, adorned with feathers and ribbons, while her face was half concealed behind an elegant mask of a swan.

"How marvellous!" Mellie gasped.

The lady nodded gracefully in acknowledgement. "You

appear lost," she said in a melodious voice. "Who are you looking for?"

"I've become separated from my company." Mellie scanned the crowd but could not find anyone.

"Who might that be?" the lady enquired.

"My mother, Lady Culkirk, my aunt." She hesitated for a moment before adding, "and the Vicomte Fouquet de Lacasse. Oh, and my sister, of course. They went ahead to his box."

"Ah!" The lady turned to face her fully. She examined Mellie from head to toe with a knowing gaze. "Your sister? She must be the vicomte's bride?"

The lady had misunderstood, but Mellie decided for the moment it would be less of a complication to leave her in the misunderstanding than to set her straight. They were masked, after all, and she wanted to remain incognito for a moment longer. "One hears much about her these days. She has been the talk of the town," the lady said.

"Rumours," Mellie interjected hastily. "It's merely rumours."

"Indeed. Rumours. Hearsay." The lady waved a gloved hand as if to dismiss them. "I usually don't pay much attention to them. And yet, as we speak, they are placing bets in the gaming room as to whether the vicomte will be left stranded at the altar yet again. The amount people are betting is unprecedented. It has never been so fantastically high. I have heard the Marquis de Montcappel went as far as betting his entire fortune; he is that confident that she will jilt him. So, tell me," the lady leaned forward to whisper, "will she?"

Mellie paled. His entire fortune? Was he mad?

"Still, one cannot help but wonder." She tapped her fan against her lips. "Why does the vicomte insist on the wedding amidst such scandal? Why endure the humiliation? When he could have any French lady at the snap of a finger." She snapped her fingers, which wasn't very loud because she was wearing gloves.

Mellie shifted uncomfortably and moistened her dry lips. "I had no idea he is so sought-after with the ladies."

"My dear!" The lady gave her an astonished look. "I can think of at least a dozen ladies who would marry him in a heartbeat."

"Are you one of them?" Mellie dared to ask.

The lady burst out laughing. "You are delightful. I would be one of them if I were free, but alas. We are only good friends, the vicomte and I."

"May I enquire as to your identity?"

The lady replied with a soft, musical laugh, "That, my dear, shall remain my secret. The unmasking hour is at midnight. Can you exercise patience until then? But come and tell me more." The lady took her by the arm and led her to a quiet alcove. "Let us continue to examine this gripping notion, for I have been pondering on it for quite a while. It is a mystery as to why he hasn't dissolved this union long ago since it has brought him nothing but trouble. Tell me, what do you think might be the reason?" She leaned forward and whispered into her ear. "Do you think he might be in love?"

Ice cold heat washed over Mellie from head to toe.

"Madly, deeply in love." The lady observed her closely. "From the very first moment he met her in Scotland."

Mellie shook her head. "You must be mistaken. They never actually met there."

"Yet how well I recall how he had set off for Scotland to meet his bride, to whom he has been betrothed since childhood, and how he was filled with great trepidation. He returned quite besotted. His betrothed is not only a beauty, but a very spirited lady with an excellent character and a heart of gold. His very words. How would he know that if they hadn't met?"

"I really wouldn't know," Mellie stammered, "when he could have met my sister to come to such a conclusion. As far as I know, there was no such occurrence, for my sister had fallen ill and was unfortunately unable to meet him. Maybe he meant another lady?"

The lady shook her head. "I am certain it was her. He's spoken fondly of her ever since. To tell you the truth, I have never seen a man so deeply in love with his bride as he. It is most unusual."

There it was, that word again. Love.

The lady sighed. "Alas, it appears to be a one-sided affair. She has not met him since, nor answered any of his letters. My poor, unhappy friend. There must be nothing worse in this world than unrequited love. They say she is certain to jilt him in a most dramatic fashion during the ceremony. Shall it really come to that?"

Mellie felt as if someone had punched her in the stomach. "I am certain my sister would not be so cruel," she began; however, the lady interrupted her.

"She wouldn't, would she? Yet, why is she dithering? If she doesn't want this union, why has she not cut the cords long ago? Why has she come here to France?" She leaned forward and whispered confidentially, "Do you think, mayhap, she might love him after all?" She tapped the fan on her arm ever so lightly. "Just a little? Might there be hope yet for my dear besotted friend?"

The lady disappeared into the crowd, leaving Mellie behind, thunderstruck.

What on earth had that been all about?

The vicomte madly in love—with her? Since years ago?

How was that possible when they'd never met?

Her mind was a whirlwind of heated thoughts as she tried to retrace all the memories, but nothing came to mind.

Spying her mother and Violet entering a nearby box, Mellie attempted to navigate her way toward them. A sudden touch on her elbow startled her.

"Melinda," a familiar voice murmured into her ear. "I have been looking for you." He spoke in English.

A thrill shot through her, and her heart pounded wildly in her chest.

He took her hand. "Dance with me."

The world around them melted away as they moved gracefully to the mesmerising melody of the cotillon. After the final tunes of the dance echoed through the room, he held her hand firmly and, without a word, guided her away from the bustling dance floor. Together, they made their way through the sea of masked revellers until they found themselves standing in a dimly lit corridor, into a shadowy nook beneath the grand staircase. In the distance, the chime of a bell signalled the approaching midnight hour.

"It's time for the unmasking," he whispered, his fingers deftly reaching for the string securing her mask. With a gentle tug, the mask slipped from her face, revealing her features bathed in the soft glow.

Simultaneously, Mellie reached out and gently removed his mask, exposing the face she had longed to see.

His face was free of any *maquillage*. He either must have removed it, or he'd never worn any to begin with, his face having been covered by the half-mask.

She cupped his face tenderly in her hands, tracing the

familiar eyebrows, the high cheeks now, the full upper lip. A peculiar weakness fluttered through her.

"Mr Brown." Her voice hitched. "I've missed you so very much."

"Philippe," he murmured. "My name is Philippe. I want to hear you say it."

"Philippe."

Without thinking, she pressed her lips against his in a sweet and shy kiss.

She felt his heat, smelled his cologne enveloping her. His arms encircled her waist, drawing her nearer with gentle urgency, pressing her close to him. He returned her kiss so gentle and full of aching longing that a tender, raw sensation unfurled within her chest, causing her knees to turn weak.

At this moment, she knew. This is what she had been wanting, this is what she'd been searching for. This closeness, this connection.

This, she thought. *Just this.*

CHAPTER 16

After that unforgettable kiss, Philippe gently guided her back to their box. She clung to his hand, telling herself that she would never let go of it willingly. However, when they reached the box, Philippe reluctantly released her hand as they were greeted by Aunt Wilma and her mother, both clearly flustered.

"'Pon my soul, now Violet has gone missing." Aunt Wilma wielded the fan back and forth in an attempt to shovel more air into their stifling box. "Really, if it's not one girl, it's the other! Lord knows where the child has wandered off to. At least you've found Melinda."

"When was the last time anyone saw her?" Philippe enquired; his features etched with concern.

"She was dancing with someone in a blue domino," Lady Culkirk replied anxiously. "I thought it was someone we knew, which is why I allowed her that one dance. But now I fear it may have been a mistake, and he may have been a stranger after all. What if she's been abducted?"

Philippe took charge, his voice firm. "I suggest Mademoiselle Finlay stays here with you in the box, while I attempt to find her."

Melinda sank gratefully into her seat; her knees unsteady, her breathing still uneven. A footman, no doubt sent by Philippe, entered, and offered them glasses of champagne, and she eagerly accepted the cool liquid. A gentleman approached their box, requesting her hand for a dance, but she declined, citing fatigue.

Half an hour later, the vicomte returned with Violet in tow.

"Where have you been, dear?" her mother exclaimed with relief.

"I was dancing, of course," Violet replied. She'd taken off her mask, revealing a flushed face and unusually bright eyes. "But I've had enough of this place. It's too noisy and stuffy, with far too many people. I can't breathe. Let's go home."

"I couldn't agree more," Aunt Wilma chimed in. "Now that the unmasking is done, much of the magic of this place has dissipated."

The vicomte escorted them out of the opera, where his chaise awaited them at the front entrance. They hadn't exchanged another word since that kiss, but as he helped her into the carriage, he briefly squeezed her hand and offered a quick smile.

Her heart somersaulted.

As the date of her wedding drew closer, Mellie found herself increasingly busy, her days filled with shopping, visits to an endless list of acquaintances and relatives, and endless hours of fitting for both her wedding dress and her courtly robe, in addition to lessons with the dance master.

The lessons with Monsieur Dupont were the worst, for the man was impossible to please.

"Elegance, more elegance!" he lamented, dabbing a perfumed handkerchief against his eyes as if watching her hurt his vision. "You cannot stomp across the room *comme une vache* with thousands of eyes upon you. You must glide. You must float! Like the wispiest dandelion in the summer breeze."

Mellie tried her best not to stomp like a cow, but to glide across the slippery parquet and float like a feathery tuft of dandelion, but her feet ached, her stomach growled, and, worst of all, her mind and her heart refused to cooperate. Ever since that kiss at the opera, her mind had been jumbled to mush, and her heart alternated between leaping and singing and floating, then trembling and longing, with anxiety pressing her down with the weight of a hundred millstones. It was enough to drive one mad.

"Wedding nerves," her aunt had diagnosed. "A perfectly normal feeling."

Was it really wedding nerves? Mellie wondered. It felt more like a malaise. A strange kind of fever that overcame her only when she thought of *him*.

She stumbled across the floor.

"There, again!" Monsieur Dupont complained. "I beg of you, Mademoiselle. Not like a cow, but like a dandelion!"

"I'd rather be a cow with all my feet firmly planted on the ground than a flimsy flower blown away by the wind," she muttered darkly. "Besides, cows are allowed to eat. Whereas I, apparently, am not."

Her stomach emitted another ungainly growl. She'd been rehearsing with Monsieur Dupont since the crack of dawn and hadn't had breakfast or lunch, not even a single sip of tea.

"That's enough for today," she declared, sitting down in the chair, and crossing her arms, a mulish expression on her face. "I refuse to do another curtsy."

"It will be a catastrophe," Monsieur Dupont moaned. "The presentation is in three days, since the queen unexpectedly insisted on having mademoiselle's presentation earlier, so now it will take place before the wedding instead of after, which is quite unorthodox and breaking etiquette, but *eh bien*, the queen is known for breaking etiquette whenever she feels like it; but as a consequence, everything has been thrown into turmoil." He turned to Aunt Wilma. "Have you nothing to say about this catastrophe, madame?"

Aunt Wilma had been sitting in an armchair, chewing an unlit cheroot, reading a newspaper, and ignoring both Mellie and her dancing master for the past few hours. "A catastrophe?" She sniffed. "Most likely. I have resigned myself to the inevitability that my niece has a tendency to attract catastrophes of all kinds, like bees to honey. One can certainly expect the formal presentation to be one as well. It is a given. Therefore, one may be agreeably surprised when it turns out to be otherwise." She placed the cheroot on an ashtray and rose from her chair. "Relax, Dupont. Melinda will do just fine. She will be the belle of the court and the darling of the queen, and everyone will be tripping over themselves to be introduced to her. Now, where is that fop of a bridegroom of hers? One hasn't seen him since that silly masked ball three days ago. Though one can hardly blame him for disappearing at a time like this. The stories one reads in the gossip columns!" She shook her head. "Preposterous." She slapped the newspaper down on the coffee table beside her, causing both Monsieur Dupont and Mellie to jump.

Mellie bit her lower lip and stared at the triangular pattern of the inlaid parquet floor. Aunt Wilma was right. She hadn't seen Mr Brown—the vicomte—that is, Philippe —for he had told her to call him by his first name, hadn't he? It was a handsome name and suited him very well, for he was, cosmetics aside, a handsome man—very hand-some, if one thought about it—those lips! Good heavens. But what had been her original train of thought? Oh yes. She hadn't seen Philippe since the ball. Since that kiss.

That kiss!

It had been all her doing. She'd kissed him.

Granted, he'd kissed her back, but she'd been the one to initiate it.

He wasn't avoiding her, was he?

He wasn't regretting it, was he?

But oh...what if he was?

And what about what the mysterious lady at the opera had said? That he was in love with her. Not just in love, but madly in love...

Surely, that couldn't be.

Why, oh why, was her treacherous heart trembling when she thought of those words and of Philippe?

She couldn't possibly be falling in love with the vicomte, could she?

Like she had with Mr Brown.

Faugh, they were the same, were they not? Had she lost her faculty of reason merely because she'd fallen in love?

She shook her head to clear her thoughts.

"What are the sheets saying now, Aunt Wilma?" she asked to distract herself from her incorrigible feelings and confusing thoughts.

159

"Nonsense. Utter nonsense. They claim the wagers placed on this wedding are the highest in the history of betting. Some ridiculous marquis or other is waging his entire fortune, only to be outdone by some duke who claims to be staking an entire estate, including a castle, not to mention gems of greater value than the crown jewels." She squinted through her quizzing glass with a frown. "Surely, that must be a bag of moonshine, but here it is, in black and white. The basic tenor being that they have all gone mad over the possibility that you will jilt Lacasse at the altar."

"I feel very sorry for *le pauvre* Monsieur le Vicomte," Monsieur Dupont declared. "To have become the butt of such cruel jokes. But just between us, I have wagered a considerable sum myself—to the contrary, of course. You would not spend hours practising the three curtsies if you were not serious about marrying him. You will not disappoint me, Mademoiselle, will you?" He rubbed his hands together. "*Enfin,* I shall be rich, very rich indeed."

Mellie considered picking up the Limoges porcelain figurine from the mantlepiece and hurling it at his head.

Aunt Wilma intervened first by rolling up the newspaper and smacking him on the head, dislodging his wig. "Fie, you should be ashamed of yourself. Be gone! And stop tormenting my niece."

Dupont scrambled out of the room, uttering apologies.

Mellie collapsed on the sofa with a moan. "This is dreadful!"

"Dinnae fash yersel, child. Don't listen to such nonsense." Her aunt patted her shoulder. "I daresay you are a tad overwrought, that's all. And you must be famished." She rang a bell.

The butler wheeled in a small table with delicacies.

"Monsieur sends his greetings and apologies for not being with you today. He has much business to attend to. He sent this." The butler placed an étagère on the coffee table. "He personally selected them from the Stohrer *pâtisserie* and insists that you must begin with the baba this time, as you haven't tried it yet; it is particularly delicious."

Mellie's face brightened as the butler presented a delicate little yeast cake soaked in wine and syrup and topped with Chantilly cream and a cherry.

It melted on her tongue. Perhaps it was the hunger, but Mellie thought she had never tasted anything so exquisite.

The butler poured some tea, and Aunt Wilma joined her, finishing an entire baba with two spoonfuls. "Not bad, but too sweet for my taste," she declared. "I prefer pineapple."

On Sunday, the day of her court presentation, Mellie was awash with anxiety. She was wearing her *grand habit de cour*, a resplendent silver-white robe of dense brocade, its short sleeves giving way to a bodice tightly embroidered with pearls and trimmed with sparkling sequins and delicate ribbons. The panniers of stiff whalebone stretched to a width she had never experienced before; her shoes, with their three-inch heels, added to her stature, as did the towering coiffure that crowned her head. Her train was fastened to the belt. Long hours had been spent shaping her hair with pomade and dusting it with powder to create an appearance befitting the gravity of the occasion.

The court dress was heavy, cumbersome, and difficult to walk in. Despite her hours of rehearsal with Monsieur

Dupont, Mellie feared she would stumble and fall at the most critical moment, disgracing them all.

The vicomte had not accompanied them in the chaise; he was already at Versailles, she was told, as the queen had requested his presence. So, Mellie found herself travelling to Versailles accompanied only by her mother and aunt.

As they passed the gilded gates of the palace, she thought she could not possibly be any more nervous than she already was. The chaise stopped in front of the Marble Courtyard, where they entered the palace. They walked up a flight of steps and passed through several chambers until they reached the Galerie des Glaces, one side of which was entirely covered in gilded mirrors, the crystal chandeliers glittering in their reflection. They passed through the enormous gallery, which was filled with some of the most glamorously dressed people Mellie had ever seen. From there, they entered another grand room. Formal presentations were customarily held in the heart of Versailles: the *cabinet du roi*.

It was a glamorous room with ornate golden-white walls lined with gilded mirrors and sparkling crystal chandeliers.

At the far end of the room, in front of the fireplace and surrounded by courtiers, sat the king and the queen.

Suddenly, all eyes were upon her.

The first formal curtsy began at the door. Then, she had to make her way across the room—giving the impression that she was floating on a cloud—pausing in the middle for the second curtsy, and then making the third curtsy in front of the queen. It was tradition that she take off her glove and bend down to kiss the hem of the queen's robe, which the queen would prevent by gracefully pulling her dress aside. She would then be introduced, followed by another three curtsies as she departed, walking backwards to the door, for it was not permissible for a subject to turn her back on the king and queen. Mellie was confident that she could manage the curtsies with elegance and finesse, but gliding backwards to find the door again without getting tangled up in her train or bumping into anyone? It was a tricky business. The entire process would be critically examined and analysed by all the lords and ladies in the room. It was daunting, to say the least. Her entire concentration was on making her way across the room and avoid trampling on her own dress or the long trains of the lady in front of her.

Then, true to her fear, it happened: her foot slipped as if the floor had been waxed with soap. Her arm flew out and she would have sprawled on the floor in an undignified manner if someone had not stopped her fall by grabbing her hand. Another arm drew around her waist firmly and stabilised her.

Her eyes shot up to meet Philippe's steady gaze. Mellie gaped at him. He was wearing a formal court dress of silk velvet, complete with the silver-hilted smallsword all courtiers were required to carry. His face was entirely without paint, blanc, or rouge. His hair was only lightly pomaded. The corner of his eyes crinkled as he smiled encouragingly.

He increased the pressure on her arm to indicate that she should continue her procession through the salon. She tore her eyes away, and together they walked towards the king and queen, who were waiting for them.

After the ritual introduction, the queen spoke. "I am pleased to finally make your official acquaintance, Mademoiselle Finlay." Her voice was melodious and very familiar, and as Mellie looked up in surprise, she met a pair of humorously twinkling blue eyes. "I look forward to welcoming you as one of my court ladies."

"You are the lady from the opera," Mellie gasped.

Marie Antoinette laughed softly. "Yes, I am. I am so sorry to have deceived you. But I deceived many that evening. My dear friend." She nodded graciously at Philippe. "May I congratulate you on your bride. She is charming."

Philippe bowed. "I am indeed the happiest man alive to have won Mademoiselle Finlay's hand in marriage."

This statement caused a stir among the crowd of onlookers, and a murmur went through the room, along with some repressed laughter and whispers.

Mellie pulled herself up and did the unthinkable. She addressed the queen. "Madame. If I may be so bold, but I would like to address your question, for you had left that night at the opera before I had the chance to answer."

The room had grown so silent, one could hear a feather drop. She took a deep breath. "You were right. He is very dear to me, my bridegroom. Not only that, but I love him with all my heart and all my soul. And I am very much looking forward to our wedding in three days." She raised her eyes and a surge of joy erupted within her as she met his gaze, brimming with love and pride.

CHAPTER 17

Of course everything had gone completely wrong, and Mellie had broken every rule of etiquette Monsieur Dupont had painstakingly instilled in her. She had cut an inelegant figure, nearly lost her balance and only managed to maintain her poise by leaning on the vicomte's arm. She'd dared to address the queen without waiting first to be addressed. ("Under no circumstances initiate the conversation; respond only when spoken to," Monsieur Dupont had implored, but to no avail.) Then she'd caused a stir by making a public declaration of love, and worst of all, she foiled the betting plans of many lords and ladies by announcing that she would marry the vicomte.

However, to everyone's surprise, the queen had appeared charmed. And even the king, a plump and altogether unremarkable figure who had been next to her, had followed the conversation with sleepy interest. At the mention of the wedding, he'd broken into a smile. "You have amused us greatly these past few weeks, mademoiselle. But of course, it is understood that the wedding will proceed. We expect it thus," he'd declared, and with a gracious nod, they were dismissed.

Her mother, however, had once more succumbed to the vapours. Another court lady fanned her and held a vial of hartshorn salt under her nose. Aunt Wilma, bless her soul, was the only one who saw nothing amiss with her presentation. "T'will do." She sniffed. "Now, let us leave this infernal place. All these people, and the stench," she wrinkled her nose, "intolerable."

Mellie would have gladly fled, except Philippe had other ideas. Without a word, he guided her through the crowds in the salons, down the stairs, and into a small antechamber. Once inside, he closed the door. "There," he said, turned to her, and without another word, drew her into his arms. "*Mon amour,*" he murmured into her hair. "My sweet love. You had to announce it to the entire court in this dramatic fashion, didn't you?"

Mellie nodded, resting her head against his chest. "I thought it was the best course of action. To put an end to all the rumours and betting once and for all." She looked up. "Do you think it worked?"

A warm smile lit up his face as he gazed down at her.

She traced his cheekbone with a finger. "Why did you decide not to wear any paint today?"

"I wanted you to see me as the man you fell in love with. Especially today. I thought showing my natural face might help ease some of your fears. And also," he hesitated briefly, "I felt it might be time to shed the mask and have people see me as I truly am. I have been wearing paste for too long. I admit, I feel somewhat uncomfortable and exposed without it. But it also feels liberating."

"Of course I prefer to see your natural face," she confessed. "But it is curious how I have grown used to the cosmetics. I do not want you to leave it off because of me. But Mr Brown—I mean, Philippe--the queen, that night at the opera, she mentioned something odd. She said we had met in Scotland, but I can't for the life of me remember that. She must be mistaken. For the only two times we were to meet, I was ill. The first time I had the influenza." She paused and said contritely, "The second time, I admit, I pretended to be ill." That had been after the incident at the opera.

He chuckled softly. "We did meet, but it was so brief it is no surprise you don't recall it. It was that time I'd travelled to Scotland for us to be formally presented."

Mellie frowned and shook her head.

"You suddenly came running from the stables with an armful of wee kittens. You ran into me. Then you offered me one." He smiled as he recalled the memory.

She stared at him, puzzled. "Why can't I remember this? I remember the kittens clearly, because the stable hand rescued them from the brook, where some heartless person tried to drown them." She furrowed her brow. "I was playing with them in the stables, correct." She tilted her head aside. "I took them outside. There was a chaise in the yard. Jake was holding the horse and another man stood beside him." She gasped. "That was you?"

"I'd just arrived. I wore a plain old travel suit and no paint. You likely mistook me for a servant. You approached the groom and said, 'Look, Jake, aren't these baby kittens adorable?' And you held a short, impassioned speech on the heartlessness of men who torture animals. Then you turned to me, saying, 'Don't you agree?' and when I agreed, you said, 'Would you like to have one?' And when you looked at me with those wonderful eyes and smiled as you handed me that kitten, I fell in love right there and then. I knew I was the luckiest fellow in the world, for you were not only beautiful, but kind and charming. Then there was a commotion at the main entrance, for your father was about to step out, and before I could utter a word to introduce myself, you fled across the meadow faster than lightning. Your father never even saw you standing there."

The memories came flooding back. The servants had been filling her ears with sordid stories of the Lacasses the night before and she'd made the decision to avoid their meeting at all costs.

"I thought you were coming out of the house with Papa," Mellie said slowly. She'd fled without her bonnet and coat to a friend's home whose estates marched with theirs, when she got caught in the rain. She arrived as a freezing, shivering bundle on the doorstep, begging to stay. Then she came down with the influenza. After she recovered a fortnight later, she'd refused to return home and begged her friend to accompany her to Inverness where she could stay with Aunt Wilma. The vicomte, in the meantime, had left, but to her great annoyance, both he and her father still insisted on the wedding to proceed.

"I thought I'd never see the day of your arrival here in France." His finger traced a gentle caress along her cheek. "Then in Calais, I found myself too cowardly to reveal my identity, and I was simultaneously charmed by Max, and how you grew to trust me as Mr Brown. You can't imagine how terrified I was of losing that trust later in Paris, when I was no longer Mr Brown."

Mellie nestled deeper into his embrace. "I apologise for all the humiliation you have endured because of me. I was such a goose. That day with the kittens, if I hadn't run away, we would've been married long ago."

"I figured you were terrified. But I was determined to

wait for you, no matter how long it took," he reassured her, his voice filled with love. "And it was worth the wait. Every minute of it."

Their lips met in a tender, heartfelt kiss.

THE WEDDING of the Vicomte Fouquet de Lacasse and his lovely bride, Mademoiselle Melinda Finlay, was the most anticipated wedding of the year. It took place in the chapel of Versailles, in the presence of the archbishop and a long list of distinguished guests. Even the queen honoured the ceremony with her presence.

Sunlight poured through the lofty stained-glass windows, engulfing the couple as if bestowing a heavenly blessing. The bride spoke her vows in a loud, clear voice, as if to declare to the world that her sentiments were unwavering and true. The bridegroom spoke his vows with equal firmness and resolution.

The vicomtesse was a vision of ethereal beauty, dressed in a simple white gown adorned with delicate Brussels lace. Orange blossoms, symbols of purity and joy, crowned her powdered hair. Her eyes brimmed with love when she regarded her bridegroom. She was, they said afterwards, the most radiant bride in all of Paris. How could there ever have been any doubt regarding her feelings for him?

"Well done," the British ambassador, Lord Stormont, told Aunt Wilma. "They seem deeply in love, the two. I am glad. Now they shall have to repeat the entire spectacle in England for their marriage to be valid under English law, eh?" He chuckled.

"Heaven help us," Aunt Wilma exclaimed. "One wedding is more than enough for me! Let it be Violet's turn next time." Then she pulled out a handkerchief and dabbed at the corner of her eyes.

Violet, who'd watched the proceedings with awe, couldn't help but shed some tears as she witnessed her sister's happiness. Her mother, not surprisingly, had fainted from sheer bliss.

The vicomte, standing tall and proud, was the epitome of courtly grace. He wore a wedding suit of shimmering silver cloth, intricately embroidered with sequins. His hair was powdered, and his face was free of paint. As they emerged from the chapel, the bells tolled.

He regarded Mellie tenderly. "The chaise awaits. We have a long journey ahead of us."

She looked at him with wide-eyed curiosity. "Don't we have the wedding breakfast next? And a concert?"

He lifted an eyebrow. "Indeed, we do. But after that, we shall embark on a somewhat different adventure."

Her curiosity piqued, she asked, "What do you mean?"

"Madame, did you not express a desire to explore Italy, Greece, and the North Pole, though the latter might pose somewhat of a challenge?" He consulted his pocket watch. "If so, time is of the essence. Shall we go?"

To the delight of the guests, Mellie, her face alit with joy, threw her arms around her husband, and kissed him. "Oh yes, let us do so, please!"

The *Georgians in Paris* frolics continue with *A Sham Betrothal!*

He can win her freedom, but can she win his heart?

With Sophie Twisden's grandmother laid up with an unidentified illness, causing them to withdraw from the Paris social scene, the pompous Sheldon Cholmeley appoints himself as Sophie's protector. Protector? Ha! More like tormentor. So when her new friend Basile de Gervain offers her the protection of his name and promises that he will not allow harm to come to her reputation when she breaks the sham betrothal and returns to London, she has little hesitation in accepting.

What once was an unthinkable notion—to align herself with a foreigner—becomes more and more the desire of her heart as she discovers how closely shared are their thoughts and sentiments. But now that it is time to leave Paris and put an end to their act, she wishes she might remain and become Madame de Gervain in earnest. But what use is it to harbour a secret hope that he will declare his undying love, when he only proposed out of pity in the first place?

BOOKS IN THE GEORGIANS IN PARIS SERIES:

The Accidental Servants by Christina Dudley
A Match Gone Awry by Arlem Hawks
The Vicomte's Masquerade by Sofi Laporte
A Sham Betrothal by Jennie Goutet

ALSO BY SOFI LAPORTE

Merry Spinsters, Charming Rogues Series

Escape into the world of Sofi Laporte's cheeky Regency romcoms, where spinsters are merry, rakes are charming, and no one is who they seem:

Miss Louisa's Final Waltz

When a proud beauty weds a humble costermonger, their worlds collide with challenges and secrets that only love can conquer.

Lady Ludmilla's Accidental Letter

A resolute spinster. An irresistible rake. One accidental letter... Can love triumph over this hopeless muddle in the middle of the London Season?

Miss Ava's Scandalous Secret

She is a shy spinster by day and a celebrated opera singer by night. He is an earl in dire need of a wife - and desperately in love with this Season's opera star.

Lady Avery and the False Butler

When a hopeless spinster enlists her butler's help to turn her life around, it leads to great trouble and a chance at love in this rollicking Regency romance.

(more to come)

The Viennese Waltz Series

Set against the backdrop of Vienna's 1814 elegance, diplomacy, and intrigue, this series twirls through the entwined destinies of friends, enemies, and lost lovers in charming tales of love, desire and courtship.

My Lady, Will You Dance? (Prequel)

A Lost Love. A Cold Marquess. A Fateful Christmas Country House Party...

The Forgotten Duke

When a penniless Viennese musician is told she may be an English duke's wife, a quest for lost love begins.

The Wishing Well Series

If you enjoy sweet Regency novels with witty banter and a sprinkle of mischief wrapped up in a heart-tugging happily ever after, this series is for you!

Lucy and the Duke of Secrets

A spirited young lady with a dream. A duke in disguise. A compromising situation.

Arabella and the Reluctant Duke

A runaway Duke's daughter. A dashingly handsome blacksmith. A festering secret.

Birdie and the Beastly Duke

A battle-scarred duke. A substitute bride. A dangerous secret that brings them together.

Penelope and the Wicked Duke

A princess in disguise. A charming lord. A quest for true love.

A Mistletoe Promise

When an errant earl and a feisty schoolteacher are snowed in together over Christmas, mistletoe promises happen.

Wishing Well Seminary Series

Discover a world of charm and wit in the Wishing Well Seminary Series, as the schoolmistresses of Bath's most exclusive school navigate the complexities of Regency-era romance:

Miss Hilversham and the Pesky Duke

Will our cool, collected Headmistress find love with a most vexatious duke?

Miss Robinson and the Unsuitable Baron

When Miss Ellen Robinson seeks out Baron Edmund Tewkbury in London to deliver his ward, he wheedles her into staying—as his wife.

NEVER MISS A RELEASE:

To receive a FREE GIFT, exclusive giveaways, review copies, and updates on Sofi's books sign up for her newsletter:

https://www.sofilaporte.com/newsletter-1

About the Author

Sofi was born in Vienna, grew up in Seoul, studied Comparative Literature in Maryland, U.S.A., and lived in Quito with her Ecuadorian husband. When not writing, she likes to scramble about the countryside exploring medieval castle ruins. She currently lives with her husband, 3 trilingual children, and a cheeky dog in Europe.

Get in touch and visit Sofi at her Website, on Facebook or Instagram!

[a] amazon.com/Sofi-Laporte/e/B07N1K8H6C

[f] facebook.com/sofilaporteauthor

[o] instagram.com/sofilaporteauthor

[BB] bookbub.com/profile/sofi-laporte

Printed in Great Britain
by Amazon

41334951R00108